HOW YELLOW FADES

By Lana Lowe

To Caty
Hope you enjoy
Love, la
Lana Lowe

Dedicated to God who gave me talent.
To my parents for always encouraging me.
Cally who showed me how to actually finish
something.
My dog Pedro that crossed the rainbow
bridge before I could finish, but who was
always keeping me company during my late-
night writing sessions.
And most of all, Madeline who suffered
reading this chapter by chapter as I worked
and was the reason I didn't give up on it.
Love you all!

Chapter 1

Yellow is far too bright a color. It doesn't suit me. There's something too... cheery about it, too out there. It stands out too much, but I guess I used to like that.

Apparently, I liked it so much that over half my wardrobe is yellow. A wall in my room is yellow.

Yellow sheets, yellow pillows, accents here and there of the obnoxious color.

Yellow.

So much yellow.

Things change.

I don't think I like yellow anymore.

"Lyric, honey!?" Serenity calls from downstairs.

Mom, I correct myself. It's weird to call someone who seems like a stranger, *mom*. It's probably weirder that I'm aware of what a mother is but don't recognize my own.

I practically trip over Godzilla, the family dog. He jumps up to follow me to the kitchen where someone has already filled his food bowl.

He's a huge thing, a grey and black Great Dane with, of course, a bright yellow collar. Since my return he's taken to guarding my bedroom door and following me around the house. The only times he's left my side is when he goes for runs with Alto or Harp.

The boys... my brothers, are already eating when I walk into the dining room. They stare. I feel like they're always staring these days. I watch as they shoot glances at each other, one kicks another under the table, there's a casual shove, and I watch a mouthed, 'stop staring.'

I must remind myself that I'm probably as much a stranger to them as they are to me. I sit down slowly next to the youngest, Harp. He smiles shyly at me. Harp's a little over a year younger than me. Even though he has a baby face, the rest of him is all lanky muscle from being involved in a bunch of sports that I barely remember.

He's not the only muscled one, either. Everyone in the family is ripped, even me. Though my muscles have gone a little soft, I guess from the past few months of not working out. Though I did start running some mornings with Alto and Harp.

"You sleep well?" One of the older ones, Cadence, who is sitting in front of me asks. We share the same honey colored eyes, naturally tan skin, and dark hair as Serenity.

No, not really. But I can't say that. I worry them enough.

Nod.

Smile.

Pretend.

What's that saying again? Fake it till you feel it. I don't know how I remember it. But that's what I do, fake a smile. What I'll

7

continue doing until the day that I can be honest with them.

Cadence is perceptive, though. He shakes his head, purses his lips and gives me a sort of hurt look, but doesn't argue with me. Instead he looks at his plate and moves the eggs around.

He would know if I'm lying, even if it's just a simple nod, because we used to be close. With only about ten months apart, the two of us were apparently best friends. The only reason we weren't in the same year in school was because my birthday falls in the winter and I wasn't at the minimum age to start school when he started.

I'm not really sure what we would be classified as now. Siblings, yes. But are we still friends? It's hard to stay close when you don't remember someone.

"Well, that's good," Serenity says as she places a plate with pancakes and eggs in front of me. She's used butter to put a smiley face on the pancakes.

Nod again. Smile again. Pretend everything is all right. But how can it be?

I don't remember.

Anything.

I am told that I am Lyric Lysanne Lyons.

I am sixteen.

I have four siblings.

It's been about four months now since the accident happened.

And now it's like I'm sleepwalking. Like I've taken a life that isn't mine. Even my name is strange. I have to remind myself of it sometimes.

Reid and Serenity are the parents.

Reid. Dad, I correct myself again. He's a musician and has some job refurbishing old guitars or building cabinets or something. I'm not sure of the details.

Whatever it is, he must make good money with it, as the house we live in is relatively nice. It's a beautiful two stories with a wraparound porch and huge fenced-in backyard.

At the moment he's talking away to one of the oldest of my brothers about something in the paper. The two oldest in our family are identical twins and I still can't tell them apart.

It doesn't help that their hair styles are similar and they both tend to dress alike. The only times its easy is when Clef is wearing his scrubs and Alto is in his exercise gear. They're the spitting image of Reid, with lighter eyes, hair, and skin than the rest of us.

Harp is the only one that is more of a mix of both Reid and Serenity, with *his* blue gray eyes and *her* dark hair, *his* build and *her* darker skin tone.

One of the twins leans back in his seat and Serenity begins chiding him, waving the spatula in the air.

Serenity is a singer.

The shared interest in music is probably why they chose music terms for all of us children as names. Serenity starts chattering with the chair leaning twin about his classes.

9

When they mention sports, I know that this one is Alto, who's studying to be a personal trainer. He boxes and has a side job teaching mixed martial arts, is what I was told. That makes the one talking to Reid, Clef. Clef is pre-med and has an internship at Silver Pines General Hospital.

I had asked Cadence why they both still lived at home since they're both in their mid-twenties, and he didn't really know either, his only guess being that it's cheaper. Clef lived in the dorms for a while and didn't like it, and Alto just never left.

The brothers are staring again. Bela, one of the family cats, rubs against my legs and starts purring. Supposedly, Reid named him after his favorite musician. One of the boys sneaks him a bit of bacon under the table and he winds around my legs before moving to them.

There's another cat somewhere that's considered solely Cadence's since it only allows him near it. He named her Perdita after his favorite Shakespeare play.

I turn and look at my plate. I can't take the almost hopeful looks anymore. It makes it harder to pretend, pretend that I don't feel guilty that I haven't remembered.

The first month was spent with days dedicated trying to trigger memories. Reid played my favorite music, Serenity cooked my favorite foods, Harp had me watch my favorite shows and movies, Cadence took me around to some of our hang out spots, Alto and Clef told me stories about me.

Things like, 'the scar on your knee is from this time when you ran right into a survey marker... one night we snuck out to the park and set off fireworks... you used to like eating frozen pudding until this time you ate entire container by yourself...'

We poured over albums and home videos.

But hours turned into days, into weeks, and soon the month was over, and I hadn't remembered. Not even a little bit.

They haven't stopped trying, but the light in their eyes is fading. I can't help but feel their disappointment like a chain keeping a hot air balloon from rising. I'm not the same. I don't know how to be.

"Hey Leary," Clef says, leaning on his elbows over the table.

Leary, their nickname for me. It came from when I was a baby and Cadence was just learning how to speak. He had trouble making the c sound in Lyric, so it always sounded like he was saying Leary and the name stuck.

"We're going out later and we wanted to know if you—"

"Long invitation short. We want you to come." Cadence interjects. Clef shoots him a look. "Whaddaya say Leary?" Cadence asks.

There isn't really a good way to say no when you have four pairs of eyes staring at you. Four people that know you better than you know yourself, since you don't know yourself anymore. It doesn't help that Reid and Serenity are giving me encouraging smiles. So, I can't exactly say no... right?

11

Chapter 2

I *should've stayed home.*
   I know, I know, I shouldn't be thinking this way when I'm out with my brothers. It's Harp's *birthday.* They didn't tell me that until we were about to leave. And it doesn't seem to bother him that I didn't know.

Everything feels wrong. And a present. I don't even have a present for him. Cadence told me not to worry about it, but I still feel bad.

I don't understand why they didn't say anything sooner, like yesterday... or last week. Maybe they were hoping I would remember? Maybe they didn't want to worry me?

It still feels wrong. What do you expect when I barely even know him now. Even if they had given me a heads up, I wouldn't have even known what to get him.

And... *he's* here too.

I ignore *him* for the moment and watch as Cadence lets Harp win a fourth time at air hockey. Cadence is hardly subtle about it, but Harp still cheers and does a dance every time like he's accomplished something great.

I turn to watch the twins at some kind of racing game. They've been at it for over an hour now. They're tied 10 to 10.

"Come on Leary, it's your turn to eat dust." Harp says with a wide grin.

Cadence shoots me a pleading look. I really want to pass, but... with the two of their stares, how can I?

I shrug and trade places with Cadence. He puts in the tokens and the machine flairs to life again.

I have the puck and drop it on the table, striking nearly too fast for Harp to block. He just barely catches it and sends it flying back. I block it with a satisfying crack and send it straight into the goal. There's a moment of silence as I exchange looks with Harp and Cadence. I'm not sure who's more surprised, me or them.

Cadence is grinning like he's got a secret, and even though it's Harp's birthday he looks ecstatic.

The game doesn't last very long. I win 2 to 7.

"And the champion returns!" Cadence says as Harp insists on a rematch.

"Pshaw, we all know the true champion is me!" Clef, or maybe it's Alto, says over Harp's shoulder. Though I can't tell them apart, I think Clef was the one wearing green earlier. He's got a smile so wide that it looks painful.

Is this a new thing? The wide smiles, or are they really that happy to be here? I don't think I've seen such genuine excitement in their faces since their hopes dwindled after my first week back from the hospital.

The other twin has his arms crossed and Cadence starts chuckling. It's easy to tell which twin won the last match.

13

Chapter 2

"You lost, foods on you." Green shirt twin
says.

The other one, wearing orange, finally grins
and nods before leaving to put in the order.
They'd been playing so long I'd practically
forgotten that they made a bet that the loser
had to pay for the pizza.

"Clef, it's your turn to lose." Harp says,
tossing the puck at him. So, green shirt twin is
Clef. I was right about something at least.

"I thought you needed to defend your title
with Leary." Cadence says.

Harp waves him away, "Like I could beat
the Master, amnesia or not." He says it so
casually, but then stops and looks at me as if
in apology. Like he's worried I'll be upset. I
just shrug.

"So... I was good at air hockey?" I decide to
play it off, like it doesn't bother me anymore,
even if we all know I'm lying.

"*Good*, that's an understatement, none of us
have ever beaten you." Clef says as he passes
some tokens to Cadence.

"Not even once." Harp adds.

"I was the one who taught you how to play."
Cadence says. He puffs his chest out proudly.

"But then the student surpassed you." Clef
says, ruffling Cadence's hair as he passes by
him. Cadence huffs at him but he doesn't
really seem that offended.

So, I was... *am* good at air hockey, I guess
that's something good to know. I watch for a
few minutes to see Harp get the first point but

then Cadence passes me some tokens and heads away to play other games.

I'm starting to have a little fun. I find I'm pretty good at a few of the other games too. I win multiple times with the fighting games and get the top score on air guitar.

We've been playing for almost an hour when it happens.

I'd been winning at the crane machine for the past 15 minutes and had more stuffed animals than I could think to do anything with. According to Cadence it was my favorite game, and obviously I was really good at it. I was just letting a maroon monstrosity drop down when there's a tap on my shoulder.

"Lyric? Lyric Lyons, right? Man is it great to run into you, haven't see you since the auditions."

The boy behind me has a punk rock look complete with ripped jeans, leather jacket, and a green Mohawk. He's attractive in a sort of unattainable way. Like a star you might watch in a movie.

"Uh, hi... do I know you?"

"Always full of jokes, you never tire do you," he turns and waves to a group of people nearby, "Mimi, it is her."

The girl that walks over is as opposite from the Asian rocker as can be. She's petite and dainty, wearing all pastels that compliment her dark skin, and carrying a tiny pink clutch in her perfectly manicured hands. She looks like a doll.

"Oh, Lyr darling! I'm so glad to see you again." She gushes and immediately wraps me in a hug. She smells of lilacs and for someone so tiny she sure is strong.

I'll admit I'm starting to get even more confused, and I'm really hoping one of my brothers will notice my predicament and sweep in to explain the whole story to them. So, that I won't have to. But none of them are in sight. Just *him.*

"The casting director has been trying to reach you for the past few weeks. You got the part!" Asian rocker says. His excitement is a palpable thing. "He said the phone kept going to voicemail, but fortunately we ran into each other, he was just about to give up and choose another Helena."

I glance around the arcade searching for one of my brothers again but it's just *him.* He's standing in the same spot, but now Evan's looking straight at me and not watching the air hockey tables anymore. He doesn't float or anything, it's almost like he's just another regular person.

I think about my phone that I've barely used since I woke up. And I've ignored any numbers I didn't recognize. I can't remember the password for the voicemail, though, so I hadn't checked them yet.

"Also, we've been unable to get a hold of Evan, do you think you could pass on the good news to him that he's been cast as Lysander." Helena and Lysander. *A Midsummer Night's Dream* pops into my head. They know me, and they know Evan... things are getting interesting.

The only thing I really hate about amnesia is having to explain it to people. Sure, it's a little sad not being able to remember my friends or family, but I don't really remember what I'm missing out on.

The doctors call it post-traumatic amnesia with a mix of retrograde amnesia. Basically, I don't remember anything before the accident that involves my personal history, but I retained my semantic memory. A fancy way of saying I remember some facts and general knowledge. I can write my name and recall the presidents, but I can't tell you who my grandmothers are.

There's not really anything they can do to fix it either. I just have to hope the memories come back, until then I have therapy and my family.

The hard part is having to tell people. To break it to them that I'm not who I used to be anymore. To see that pitying look, to hear them say, 'I'm sorry,' as if they had something to do with it.

"I think I'm going to have some bad news for you." I go into my whole spiel about how I suffered a head injury in a freak accident. Freak accident is the nicer version of horrendous car crash.

Evan and I are lucky we survived. The others in the car... they weren't so lucky. I go on to tell how I lost my memories. At first, they seem to think I'm joking, but then I get to the bit about Evan.

See the real reason I try to ignore Evan hovering nearby isn't because he's a creepy stalker or anything like that. No, it's a little stranger than that.

"And I'm really sorry to have to be the one to tell you this but Evan is in a coma at Silver Pines General Hospital right now, has been since the accident."

Chapter 3

When I'm finished with my story the rocker and baby doll look like they're going to be sick, both becoming a little green.

The boy squeezes one of the girl's hands and it looks like she might faint. I know it's probably not every day you meet someone you know that can't remember you. Or hear about someone else you know in a coma, especially as young as we all are.

I look past them towards Evan who's moved now to hovering behind the foosball table.

"Oh dear, oh dear, you poor things." My story earns me another hug from Mimi and then a friendly pat from the rocker. Neither give me those pitying looks, a little shock and confusion but no pity, and I feel a wave of relief.

"I'm so sorry to hear that Lyric. I really am... I guess I should officially introduce myself then," he holds his hand out for me to take, cracking a wide grin. "Hei Daniels, actor." He says the name like one would say hey, and I wonder how he spells it.

The girl gives me a smile that could make flowers bloom. "Mimi Rockley."

After a few more moments of talking we move to the group of people that Mimi came from and Hei explains that they're some of the other actors and crew. Hei was cast as Puck and it turns out that Mimi, for as dainty as she is, isn't actually an actress.

"I get stage shy." She explains. "But I just love the theater, so I hop around in the back and every now and then I play extras and nonspeaking parts."

"She's being humble. She's the assistant stage manager." One of the other girl's chimes in. Mimi waves her hand as if this isn't a big deal.

"Only for this production. The last one I oversaw props, and before that I did lights." Mimi explains.

"She impressed the stage manager because she's so adaptable." The girl adds, beaming at Mimi.

"More like her Aunt is one of the producers, so she gets to do whatever she wants," another girl says. The first girl throws a packet of ketchup at her.

"Mimi earned those positions, she works harder than any of us." Hei says in her defense. There's a collective agreement from everyone else.

The rest of the group make their introductions so fast it's a little hard to follow.

There's a Lenard, Rochelle, Patricia, Martin, Harper, Robbie, Tonya, and a Candace, but who is who and what they did, I can't really remember.

They're an eclectic bunch though. I wonder if I fit in with them.

"Rehearsals don't start for another month. Our director wanted to let the props and set designers finish before they started. Our first read through hasn't even been scheduled yet. So, there's still time for you to accept the part and start studying lines." Hei says.

"No, she should probably pass, she's been through an ordeal after all." A brown skinned, pink haired girl says. Mimi throws a fry at her.

"You're just saying that because you're the understudy." Mimi turns to me. "Don't pay any attention to Candy, Lyr. Even if you don't get your memories back you can still do the part if you want." She gives me a little pat on my shoulder.

"Yeah, and you'd make a great Helena. I saw your audition; you were amazing with that monologue." A chubby little redhead says from across the table. If I'm remembering correctly, she's Rochelle. And she's playing Titania.

"Umm... maybe I should think about it for a while." This must've been something the old me was really interested in if I auditioned for a lead, but I find it strange that none of my family mentioned it to me. On top of not telling me about Harp's birthday, I wonder what else they're omitting.

"Don't think too long or I'm snatching the part for myself." Candace says, ducking another fry from Mimi. She grins and gives me a wink, but I have a feeling that she's serious in hoping I don't take the part.

"Don't pay her any mind." Hei says around a bite of burger. His phone buzzes and he glances at it, making a face as he turns back to his food.

We spend a little bit of time talking. Everyone is eccentric and outgoing enough that I don't have to say much. Perhaps it's because the majority of them are actors and good at reading people, but they don't pester me with questions about my accident, nor do they tell me about me.

For the first time in months I'm sitting down with people who knew the old me, but I'm not hearing all sorts of stories about me. Nor am I pretending to ignore looks of guarded hope.

They just ramble about all sorts of things, and I can see why I probably liked them. It's barely been thirty minutes, but I feel like I've known all of them longer than anyone, even my family, and like we'd spent days talking.

"Well, we need to be heading home, but it was good seeing you again Lyr," Hei says standing up and slinging a duffle bag over one shoulder. Mimi joins him and gives me another quick hug and waves goodbye with the stuffed animals I'd given her.

She gushed so much about how awesome it was that I'd won so many. And as good at the game as I am, I really don't have a use for colorful stuffed creatures. Not to mention that machine was filled with strange monstrosities like pink elephants and turquoise turtles.

"Be sure to call us to hang out!" Mimi calls, waving her pink jewel encrusted phone at me. Just before they leave Hei's phone goes off again and he and Mimi exchange a tense look.

I'm curious, but I don't know them well enough to ask what's wrong.

Evan's standing beside the others and waving too, as if he's about to leave with them. Rochelle gives me a hug also and even Candace surprises me with one.

"Your audition really was marvelous," she says. "I won't say that I'd be heartbroken if you didn't take the part, but for what it's worth, memories or no, I bet you'll still do it justice. So, think on it." And then she skips out with the others, leaving me with a bittersweet feeling.

Not long after the group leaves, Cadence appears out of nowhere.

"There you are. The pizza's ready."

Three large pizzas covered in what looks like every meat there is, practically take up a table to themselves. There's also a fourth pizza loaded with veggies and a fifth dripping cheese.

The boys have pushed two tables together and as soon as I'm seated they begin what looks like a sort of war to grab slices as quick as they can.

"I'm not going to lose a hand if I try to get a piece, am I?" I ask Cadence whose plate has four slices on it and he's already halfway through another.

"Grab it while you can." He says around a mouthful of pizza.

"Seriously, are you having a competition to see who can eat the fastest?" I ask, glancing at the twins who seem to be doing just that. For guys in their twenties, they really don't act any older than the rest of us.

"Come on Leary, eat. I bet I can eat more than you." Harp says from beside me. I arch a brow at him, wondering why I'm suddenly raring to go in for the challenge.

It's something about the way he says it that triggers, not a memory, but a feeling. The others all stop, mouths still full, pizza hanging in the air as they stare at me.

"What do I get when I win?" I ask. I reach to fill my plate with as many slices as possible and the competition is on.

* * *

"Seriously, I still can't believe you ate that much pizza." Cadence says, practically wiping tears from the corners of his eyes from laughing so hard. It's been hours since we left the arcade, each of us going to finish tasks on Serenity's checklist while Harp went to meet a few friends that had gifts for him.

"Hey, I won! So, there." I stick my tongue out at him. I can't believe I ate 14 slices of pizza either. But I beat Harp who nearly puked after his ninth piece. And since I won, I get to choose the movie we watch tonight.

I wish I actually remembered what I liked though. I know from some of the ones Harp had me watch that I had a wide range of interests. My favorites ranging from really awful horror films, to action movies, comedies and musicals, and a few obviously low budget fantasy movies. Surprisingly there wasn't any romance in there. Harp said most romances bored me and I'd usually fall asleep during them.

"True, true, though if Alto was against you, then he would've won." Cadence says.

"So... I met some people that knew me." I say casually, changing the subject, as Cadence checks the little grocery list in his hands.

"Oh, really? Awesome. Hey, grab that bag of brown sugar, will you?" I pass him the brown sugar and he crosses it off. "We just need to grab the eggs and heavy whipping cream and then we're done." He walks off, pulling the buggy behind him.

"They mentioned that they were part of a theater company." I add. Cadence is walking so fast I have to practically run to keep up.

"Oh, really?" Cadence asks as he makes a beeline for the milk section. "You and Evan were in theater club a few years back, must've been them.

"No, um, outside of school in some little community theater. So, I was really interested in acting?" Fishing isn't working with Cadence at the moment, so I decide to go the direct route.

He plants a gallon of heavy whipping cream in the buggy and turns to stare at me. I can't comprehend why we need that much heavy whipping cream, but I'm not planning on asking.

"Where'd that question come from?" Hello, wasn't he listening?

"The people I met, they're part of a community theater called The Rising Eclipse... they said I auditioned for a part. One of the leads." Cadence nearly drops the eggs he's now holding.

"I guess this is news to you, huh?" He places the eggs in the buggy without a word. We're almost to the checkout register before he turns to look at me again.

"I guess... I mean I knew you liked to act. Like I said, you and Evan were in the theater club back in middle school. Heck, you met Darryl when we were in elementary school because of a play... but you never... you never told me about auditioning for the community theater... I didn't... I didn't know." The look on his face almost makes me feel guilty, even though I have no idea why I would've hidden this from him

"Maybe I was planning on surprising everyone?" Cadence nods, his tense look decreasing a bit.

"That sounds like something you'd do. You know you used to be practically obsessed with trying to surprise people..."

He starts telling me about how I tried to plan surprise parties all the time with random themes like a moustache day and the paint party that nearly dyed the back-porch purple. I only half listen.

So, despite how close Cadence and I supposedly were, there were things that even he didn't know about me. At least that means that the rest of the family probably isn't hiding things from me. I'm not sure if I feel reassured by that thought or not.

Outside the ominous clouds that had been looming since morning have finally decided to unleash a torrent of rain.

"I'll get the car, wait here." Cadence says before dashing out into the downpour. I watch as he splashes across the parking lot, the rain is so heavy that he disappears from sight after a moment.

"Lyric? Lyric!?" A voice is yelling nearby. I turn to see a woman, most likely the twins age, heading towards me. When she's under the awning she shakes out her umbrella and grins at me.

"It is you, I haven't seen you in quite a while." She says, giving her umbrella another shake. She's got long auburn curls that trail halfway down her back and beautiful caramel colored skin. She looks like she could be a model. Everything about her is pristine from perfectly manicured hands to a dress that looks like it came straight from a catalogue. I'm about to do my whole amnesia spiel when she offers me a hand.

"My mistake, you do not remember me, correct? I had heard, you know, but it is still rather surprising in person." I take her hand and she gives it a firm shake.

"Analise Tisby, it is a pleasure to see you again Lyric." She has this formal way of talking that makes me think that English isn't her first language and she pronounces her name with a particular flourish, drawing out the syllables so it sounds more like, 'On-uh-lease Tiz-bee.'

"So, uh how do you know me?" The more I meet strangers that know me the less polite I've started to become.

"Your accident... how are you doing darling?" She asks instead of answering.

"I guess I'm as good as I can be. So, who are you again?"

"Oh, you haven't heard about me, have you? That is understandable, well the simplest explanation is that I—"

There's a honk as Cadence pulls the car up and then he's jumping out of the car.

"What the heck are you doing here?" He says pushing in between Analise and me. It only takes a moment for me to realize he's not talking to me.

"It is a public store, is it not?" Analise says, not the least bit flustered. She inspects her nails as if she's suddenly bored with being here.

Cadence, on the other hand, looks crazed. His face is bright red, his hair plastered to his forehead, drops of water trickle from his clothes.

"Yes, right, it's plenty public." He spits out. He turns to me. "Lyric, get in the car, I'll put the bags up."

"We were just talking. She said she knows me."

Cadence turns back to Analise. "You've done enough, haven't you? Why can't you just leave our family alone?"

"I was simply introducing myself to your sister, since she does not remember me anymore, I cannot even make small talk with her now?" She arches a brow at him. "We used to be friends after all."

Cadence's fists ball up at his sides. So, I'm guessing something happened between them?

"No, not after what you did. So, leave us alone. Lyric. Get. In. The. Car." I've never seen him so angry, then again, I only remember the worrier of the past few months that's been doing everything in his power to make me happy, in an effort to bring back my memories.

That Cadence hovers behind me like a shadow, constantly bringing me snacks and offering to drive me around with no destination in mind. This Cadence... is something else.

"Cadence... I-I think you should calm down." I reach for his hand, but he shrugs me off. His fists are clenched so tight the knuckles are white.

"So, no one mentioned me at all? That's hurtful Cadence, very hurtful. After all I was a big part of the family." She was?

"Not anymore, so leave us the heck alone. Don't come near any of us again, and don't talk to Lyric again. Lyric. Car. Now."

"You're not even going to tell her who I am are you?" She asks.

She's riling him up. Instead of just turning and leaving she's trying to get a reaction out of him. I wonder why.

"Lyric! Car." Cadence says through his teeth. Some sort of gut feeling tells me I shouldn't leave just yet, Cadence is pissed, and Analise is enjoying it.

"Cadence..." I reach for him again and this time he lets me grab his hand, some of the tension leaves his shoulders. He's staring at the ground now, as if even looking at Analise is too much for him.

"Yes Cadence, perhaps you should calm down for your sister's sake, she's been through quite the ordeal, has she not?"

I'm not sure what's going on, but that comment gets to me. There's venom in it. Before Cadence can react, I step forward.

"That's enough!" I have to stop myself from slapping her and I'm not really sure why. "Don't you talk to him like that."

Her eyes widen a bit as if I've shocked her for some reason.

"I see the two of you are as close as ever, memory or no. Fine, I can take a hint," she spins so fast her hair whips out behind her in a flurry of curls. She stops at the door, twirling her umbrella in her hands. "Oh, Cadence, do be a dear and send Clef my love."

With that she sashays out of sight.

"That witch." Cadence spits out. "She hasn't changed a bit."

"Ok, there, Mr. Hyde, care to explain?"

He shakes his head. Slowly uncurls his fists and points to the buggy.

Chapter 3

"You know that's your favorite movie." He says with a sigh. I only know that because Harp had me watch it.

When I don't respond, Cadence let's out another sigh, running his hand through his wet hair.

"Not yet. Get in the car, please."

Chapter 4

"It's been ten minutes, are you going to tell me what that was about or not?" Cadence pulls the car into a Sonic parking lot. He hasn't said a word the entire time, but I can tell he's agitated, his shoulders are all tense and he's practically squeezing the blood out of his hands on the steering wheel.

"Seriously Cadence, why are you stopping, Serenity's making dinner, and there's heavy whipping cream in the backseat."

I'm glad he seems too distracted to address the fact that I still can't say Mom when referring to Serenity. I know it's been bugging the whole family, but it just feels weird.

"It's fine. I placed it next to the frozen peas and ice cream, and I'll explain everything... after milkshakes." He rolls down the window to order.

"A large pineapple chocolate shake and a large strawberry peanut-butter shake, extra whip cream and cherries on both."

I can't hear the tinny reply very well, but Cadence pulls out his wallet and starts counting out exact change.

"You didn't ask me what I wanted." I point out. He looks up for a moment before continuing to count out his cash.

"I know what you like. I got your favorite."
He gives me a sideways glance. "Well, used to
be your favorite, I guess we'll find out."

"Both those combinations sounded
disgusting."

"Believe me, you loved it." I sigh, rolling my
eyes. But the tension has left his shoulders a
bit, so I can't really stay irritated. A few
minutes later there's a tap on the window and
our shakes are handed in.

"So, which of these weird concoctions is
mine?"

"The pineapple chocolate," I make a
gagging face and he chuckles. "Just give it a
try."

He takes a long draw of his own disturbing
drink and relaxes into his seat. I take a
tentative sip and find it doesn't taste nearly as
bad as it sounds, but I don't want to give him
that satisfaction just yet, so I make a grossed-
out face. His expression crumbles a bit and I
can't hold the fake disgust.

"Cheer up, it's delicious."

"Oh, now you're just being cruel." But he's
laughing and so am I.

"Sooo... why'd you go all crazy back there?
You about flipped out on her."

Cadence takes another long draw of his
shake and then turns in his seat to face me.

"Ok... where to begin... see umm... uh, well
you see—"

"How about you just start with how we know
her."

Chapter 4

"Ok, yeah, that's a little easier. So, up until a few months ago... not even two weeks before your accident Analise was Clef's fiancée." Okay, so *not* what I was expecting.

"What, seriously?" That explains a little, but still not why Cadence was ready to explode on her for talking to me.

"Yeah, they hadn't been dating long, it was actually the cause of a bit of discontent."

"So... I take it that I wasn't all buddy buddy with her?"

"No, actually the two of you were close."

"Okay you lost me now." Cadence's phone beeps and he glances at it.

"It's Mom, guess we gotta head back," he focuses on getting the car out of the lot without comment.

I'm thinking that I'm going to have to start interrogating him when he lets out a long sigh. "You hated her actually, you and Mom were the only ones that saw through her, she had the rest of us practically fooled."

Cadence lets out a bitter laugh. "You said she had to be hiding something to want to get married that quickly."

"So, how long did they date?"

"They'd only been official for two months, but they'd sort of known each other for six. They intern with each other at the hospital. Clef was smitten after she suddenly confessed to him one day. Heck, we all were." Well, she *was* gorgeous, can't argue with that.

"So, Serenity and I weren't fans of her... and we were right? What happened? Was it my accident?"

"Yeah, you and Mom were both right, she had a secret, and no it wasn't your accident that caused the breakup... she was cheating on him." Cadence pauses to take another sip of his shake. "He... Clef caught her in the act, at work, and cut her off. It was with someone else at the hospital."

Ouch, now I wanted to rip the girl's hair out. That certainly explained Cadence's hostility.

"Poor Clef, how'd he take it?" Cadence let's out another bitter laugh.

"About as well as one can. He's sworn off women for the time being apparently. To be honest she was the first serious relationship he'd had. Clef has always been too focused on his schoolwork to date, and so she did a number on him. She keeps trying to get him back too, which isn't helping the situation, and he's actually considered getting a restraining order." Cadence gives me a side glance.

"He gave her a second chance before you were released from the hospital, but he said he just couldn't bring himself to trust her again or even see her the same, and so he broke it off. I honestly don't think it was just the cheating, he realized how narcissistic she was. For instance, she got angry at him for canceling a date to check on you." Cadence brushes his wet hair back again.

"She seems to think if she bugs him enough he'll relent and give her one more try, though."

"Goodness, and no one thought to mention this?" Cadence shrugs.

"Didn't think it was that important, what with trying to help you remember and all, but I bet anything that that narcissistic witch thinks that if she can get his amnesiac sister to be friendly again, that that's the best way to get back in his good graces."

Yeah, I'm *definitely* going to rip her hair out the next time I see her.

"If I hated her then why did I befriend her? Obviously, she didn't get the memo that I couldn't stand her." Cadence chuckles.

"Well, you were keeping your enemies close. I believe your exact words were, 'I refuse to let that viper sink her fangs into Clef.'"

I sit back and sip my shake for a moment mulling it over. Here was a side to me that hadn't been mentioned before, a side that was calculating and protective. I'm not sure why, but it's a side that I want to get to know more.

"But she never told you about her guy on the side." Cadence says.

Well, that was obvious, no matter how close you are, or think you are, you don't tell a person's sister that you're cheating on them.

"But enough of this," Cadence says as the car pulls into the driveway. "Let's just focus on celebrating Harp's birthday..." He puts the car in park and turns to look at me.

I can read his expression before he says a word and I'm already nodding as he asks, "And let's not mention running into Analise to Clef."

* * *

"Oh goodness dearie, I'm so sorry, I didn't see you there." Evan's grandmother takes a step back and gives me a friendly pat before she looks up at me. "Oh, Lyric dear! So, good to see you again, I was just heading home for the day, do stop in some time for tea, will you?"

I nod, a grin splitting my face, it's so hard not to smile around this old lady. She crushes me in one of those bone-jarring hugs, the smells of lavender and mint surrounding her.

"I'm sure Evan will be pleased to hear from you." She dabs at her eyes with a blue silk handkerchief.

Evan's grandmother is everything that you'd expect a doting grandmother to be except she doesn't look the part.

She's definitely not the doddering old lady type that wears baggy sweaters and floral prints, and despite the accident and everything that's happened it seems that she's adopted me as her own. Or rather my whole family has been adopted by her.

She's been over for dinner several times since the accident, and from my understanding this is a normal occurrence. She even stopped in for Sunday breakfast a couple of times, which has consistently produced enough food to feed the entire neighborhood.

"I see you dyed your hair again Mama Etta?" She gives me a wide smile and ruffles her newly blue curls.

"Ah yes baby, I felt like it was a blue kind of week." When I'd first met her, she had bright purple hair and when I'd asked about it she'd given me a deep chuckle and responded with, 'Once you get to my age it's about making the most of every little thing, or you'll just get more wrinkles.'

She pulls out a handful of caramel candies and hands them to me. "You look well?" It's not so much a statement of fact as it is a question.

I'm about to spill my guts on every tired and depressing thought I'm having, she's just that easy to talk to, but her head bobs up and down as if she already knows what I'm going to say, and she pats my cheek.

"It'll get better, dearie. You're still young and spry," I can already feel tears prickling the corners of my eyes. It's so hard to keep all my feelings bottled up around this woman. Tears that aren't so much sadness as they are frustration. "Ah baby don't do that now. You're too pretty and young to let that eat away at you. Come here, dearie." She pulls me in for another hug, practically smothering me. "Now, now, give us a smile, humor the old woman, will you?" She pats my head and gives me a goofy grin until I start giggling.

"Now there's that pretty smile. Now you be nice to my boy, and I expect to see you for tea soon." With that said, she wobbles off, surprisingly fast for a lady with a cane.

That hobble is one of the few things that reveal her age. For a woman in her seventies she's remarkably young in personality and looks.

Perhaps the only thing that's changed about Evan since I first came to visit him is that his chestnut hair is now brushing the tops of his shoulders where it once was barely touching his ears.

It's funny, and maybe a little sad that I've seen him so many times over the past few months that I have his face memorized, but I can't remember what colors his eyes are.

The familiar buzzing and beeping of machinery greets me, and Evan in his green hospital gown amidst the bland white sheets.

"It must be odd, huh?" I say sitting down beside his bed as way of greeting. "Odd that I come to visit you even though I don't remember you, isn't it? Your hair is getting longer."

I take one of his hands in mine and give it a squeeze, partly to remind myself that this is the real Evan, not the spirit I always see, but also to resist the urge to run my hand through his curls that I get every time.

Sometimes he squeezes back, but today there's no reaction. The first time his hand moved in mine I ran to the nurse's station, ecstatic, thinking he was waking up, but apparently, it's just a sign that he is slightly conscious. There's hope that he'll wake up, but it's still rather slim.

"I wish I remembered you. I wish you'd wake up... okay, I know... I know I say the same things every time, but it's hard, you know?"

I can't resist the urge anymore, I brush his hair off of his face, pulling apart some of the curls. I wonder if anyone would object to me braiding it? Well, it's not like he's going to wake up. And it wouldn't be the first time I did it. I start working braids though his hair, it gives me something to do with my hands and it's calming.

"Then again maybe it doesn't matter whether you're awake or not. I'm not going to remember you. Sometimes I think I won't ever get my memories back, but sometimes that... well, it doesn't bother me as much as it probably should. If I don't remember, it's not like I know what I'm missing, but the looks in everyone's faces... I wonder if you'd give me that same look," I let out a laugh.

"I bet you would, and you'd tell me stories about me, just like the rest."

But there's a difference. Evan wouldn't just tell me stories of me, he could tell me about the accident, something that no one else seems to know the specific details of.

And that might be part of the reason I like to talk to Evan and visit him even though I don't really know him. Maybe I hope that one day I'll suddenly remember the details, or perhaps he'll wake up and tell me everything. But there's another reason, besides just our connection with the accident, being with Evan is... easy. There's no expectations when I'm with him, no disappointment each moment that I don't remember. It relaxes me.

"So, I almost forgot to tell you about Hei and Mimi." I've braided about a third of Evan's hair at this point. "Harp's birthday was a few days ago." I pause to work my fingers through a knot in his curls, trying to be careful of pulling too hard. It might almost be humorous that I'm trying not to hurt him when he probably wouldn't wake up if I did.

"I met some people that knew us. We act, and I guess we're good at it. We got cast as two of the leads. They want to come visit you soon." The knots out and I comb through the strands before carefully plaiting them.

"I went out for frozen yogurt with them yesterday. They're... interesting, but they don't know about the accident. I think there's something else going on with them too, but maybe I just don't know them well enough yet, and the weird looks at one another every time Hei's phone goes off is normal."

I'd worried that hanging out with them again might be awkward, but it was just as fun as at the arcade. They're just really easy to get along with. And even though they're a couple I didn't feel like a third wheel or anything.

I finally pull my hands out of Evan's hair, momentarily trying to decide whether to leave the braids in or not.

"You would know, wouldn't you? But I guess it won't be that easy..." I sit for a moment and then reach to undo the braids. I yank my hands away at the sound of people in the hall, almost afraid of being caught.

"Is this the right room?" A guy's voice. I don't recognize it. But there's a twinge in my gut, that makes me feel like I should.

"Maybe, I don't know, it's not like there was a specific number in the article or that letter." A girl's voice... it's familiar somehow.

"Should we just leave? Maybe this is a bad idea?" The guy again, I wonder if they're friends of Evan's. I cross over to the doorway, listening to the voices argue, still trying to place the girl's voice.

"Okay, okay, you're right, we should just leave then." My mind is reeling. No! They can't leave... what if... what if they know something?

I yank the door open at that thought, but the hall is empty. Completely empty.

There's no way they could've walked off that fast. I fall back into the room, practically collapsing in the chair by Evan's bed.

"I think I'm going crazy." And then another thought hits me. I know why I know that girls voice, why it was so familiar.

It was my voice.

Chapter 5

"**L**yric I made us some tea to go! Come on already!" Cadence yells from downstairs. Tea, another thing that's different now. The me before didn't like tea, but I've developed a taste for it, something that has pleased Cadence greatly.

Apparently, he'd been trying to get me to develop a taste for tea since he discovered that he liked it more than coffee. The whole tea versus coffee is actually an interesting debate between everyone in the family.

"Lyric! Hurry up! It's not like I can leave without you, your appointment is first!" Cadence yells at me again. I sigh, grabbing a yellow cardigan and rushing downstairs to meet him. I nearly trip over Godzilla again. I give him a pat and leave my door open for him as I pass by.

He gives me a mournful awoo as I leave. He really doesn't like it when I leave now. Even though he's supposed to be the families dog, it seems like he's most attached to me. Serenity said I was the one who picked him and named him, and he was so little when we got him that I bottle fed him.

It's been over a week since I visited Evan. I've convinced myself that I must be going crazy. Not counting hearing my own voice outside of Evan's hospital room, I've heard it three other times in various places.

Always so casual, as if it could be someone else, but whenever I look there's never anyone there. That, on top of seeing Evan's ghost, and the nightmares I never remember the details of, I'm afraid of what might happen next.

Cadence has taken to staring at me and asking what's wrong, but it's not like this is something I can just blurt out. He'd probably have me committed. Instead he seems to be convinced that I'm getting sick and has taken to loading me with vitamin C, and keeps offering to make me chicken noodle soup.

I haven't really decided if it's endearing or irritating yet. Downstairs Cadence passes me a to-go mug and an orange.

"Seriously?" I ask him. I reach past him to trade the orange for a couple of granola bars and he sighs.

"You should eat the orange. It's good for you."

"Yeah, yeah Mom. Whatever you say." Cadence let's out a huff but doesn't say anything else as he follows me to the car. We're already late, so it's not like he has time to argue.

When we reach the car, I see he's grabbed the orange and he places it in my lap before starting the car.

"For later." He says with a slight smirk. I roll my eyes but shove the orange into my bag, a yellow eyesore, before sitting back to enjoy my granola bar breakfast.

We're heading to my weekly therapy session, and of course what better place to go for someone going crazy.

I wonder if the therapist will just sense the loony in me, or maybe crazy has a smell? Guess we'll find out. Then again, I don't think she's noticed anything off yet, and well, she's a little eccentric herself.

Since the accident the entire family has started therapy. The doctors suggested it for me, to help regain my memories, but I guess because of the trauma Reid and Serenity thought it would be good for everyone.

Mine and Cadence's sessions are always Monday mornings, Harp goes in the evenings when he finishes his baseball practices, while Reid, Serenity, and the twins have theirs on the weekends so that they don't have to rush over after work.

Carren is not your typical looking therapist or typical anything, really. She's got a hippy look to her and her building is covered in tapestries, hanging lanterns, and floor pillows. There's a large fountain of a dragon curled around a castle, water trickling from the turrets and steam emitting from the dragon's nose.

On the opposite end of the room is a coy pond, the fish swimming over a brightly marbled pool, a yin and yang symbol shining on the tiles. A large sign hangs over the pond, telling visitors not to throw coins in, because they can be toxic to the fish.

To complete it all is a statue of a big bellied Buddha that greets us at the door. Cadence heads over to a floor cushion in the lobby and starts reading a book he brought with him as I make my way to Carren's office.

"You're just on time Lyric!" Carren says, rushing over to hug me. I'm not really sure about the proper etiquette for therapy sessions, but I'm betting Carren doesn't practice most of it.

At least she doesn't care about being a few minutes late. The first time we were late she'd said the same thing and I'd corrected her, only for her to give me a mini lecture about how time is all an illusion, and then something about it being a social construct to keep us constrained and from truly taking the time to enjoy our day-to-day lives. I'm not really sure I fully agree with her about the irrelevant nature of time and all, but it sure made things easier when we were late more often than not.

I'd looked Carren up after our first session and she is indeed a licensed professional, if a little light on the professional part. She also happens to be a fortune teller in her spare time, reading auras, and palms, and tarot cards and all that, which might be another factor of the hippy vibe, metaphysical, I correct myself.

I'd found that term on her website and was still getting used to using it. I think maybe she just has more leeway because she's her own boss. And the new-age thing must be trendy enough to keep her in business since she's been doing therapy sessions and readings for three years now.

Plus, my entire family loves her, there's just something so warm and relaxing about being around Carren. She's so easygoing and sweet.

Her office is heavy with the scent of jasmine and vanilla and has an Arabian Nights feel, complete with a draped ceiling and a little cushioned seating area in the floor at the center of the room. In the far corner is a settee and a plush recliner, perhaps for those that won't or can't sit in the floor seating. I plop on a floor poof and lean back into the wall, kicking my sandals off. Carren herself is always barefoot, a little anklet of bells chiming as she closes the door.

"So, tell me how this week has been? Anything new?" Carren asks as she lights the candles around the room, her purple skirts swishing around her feet.

The answer is usually no, because of course I'm not going to mention the voices, nor have I ever told her about Evan's ghost. Though Carren being as eccentric and open minded as she is would probably believe me without thinking I'm crazy. It's still not something I really want to share, but this time I realize I do have some things to share.

"I do have some news... kind of. I met some people that knew me and Evan."

She's finished lighting the candles now, she claimed they helped to purify any negative energies in the air. They always smell like fresh laundry and sometimes cookies, so I never complain.

She motions for me to continue as she takes the seat in front of me.

"Well the first two were from a theater company. Apparently, we like to act and auditioned for two of the leads, and we'd gotten them."

"So, did this bring back any memories? Perhaps other things you may have acted in."

"That's the strange part, no one in the family knew I auditioned for it, nor did any of them know that I was that into acting in the first place. Like Cadence mentioned I'd been in an acting club before but he said he thought it was just a passing interest. And Serenity and Reid said that I hadn't been in a play since elementary school, at least not that they knew of." I'd asked everyone else the next day. And even Serenity had been surprised.

"I see you're still calling your mother by name, have you worked any on that?" She asks. I shake my head. I still can't bring myself to call her Mom. It just doesn't seem right. Like a lie.

Thankfully Carren doesn't push the subject.

"Hmm, so you discussed the acting with everyone and no one knew, perhaps you were planning to surprise everyone? You told me before that your family keeps bringing up a journal that you used to carry around a lot. Have you been able to find it yet? Maybe it would have some clues." Carren suggests.

That's not the first time she's suggested finding my journal, nor the first time I'd thought of it. As soon as Cadence had mentioned it I'd searched all over my room, but it's been months and I still can't find it. All that my brothers could tell me was that I always hid it, and never in the same spot. I shake my head no.

"And the others you met?" Carren says easily diverting off the glum subject.

"An ex of one of my brothers. They were engaged, but no one thought to even mention her."

"And did she jog any memories?"

I shake my head again. The session is starting to become a repeat of many of our sessions. She asks questions and I provide her with no results.

She'd convinced me to take up yoga, saying that the flow of positive energy would possibly allow the memories to come back. I'm fairly certain that no real human can do yoga, either that, or humans with iron wills. The concentration alone nearly put me to sleep, so I promptly quit after my first try.

Carren continues to ask about my week, so I tell her about my visit with Evan and running into his grandmother again. I tell her about winning air hockey against Harp, she refers to that as muscle memory. Somehow, we end up back on the confrontation with Analise.

"I don't really know what came over me, but I wanted to slap her so badly after she upset Cadence like she did."

"It's not unusual to want to protect those we love, even if you don't remember that you love him." She responds.

The session winds down and she tells me to try harder to find my missing journal. Then I trade places with Cadence.

While Cadence is in his session I decide to walk to the library down the street, sending him a quick text to tell him where I'll be.

The library is old and antique looking with two stone lions guarding the doorway. It's strange that I can remember that this library has a decent selection of books but can't remember what genres I used to like or even what my favorite book is.

Rounding a section of mystery books, I see Evan. He's not looking at me this time, but examining the books in the section, he reaches toward one, and I'm kind of curious to see if his hand will go through the book.

"Can I help you find anything?" A voice says from behind me. I jump, startled, and turn to see a pile of out of control brown obscuring a girl.

A mouse comes to mind while looking at her. She's short, probably not even five feet tall and chubby. She's got a handful of books about to fall out of her hands and I can see a cart nearby.

"Uh... no, just looking. Thanks though." I turn to see that Evan has disappeared and the idea hits me.

"All right, well let me know if you need help finding anything." The girl says as she turns to leave.

"Actually... the supernatural." I swallow, trying to get the words out faster than my mouth wants to work. "What books do you have about the supernatural?"

Evan's obviously a disembodied spirit. Maybe if I research ghosts, I can figure out how to help him.

"You might be able to find a few in our teen section." She points to a nearby row of books.

"No... umm ghost stories. I'm looking for ghost stories. Or stuff about ghosts and..." I stop, trying to think of the best way to word this without sounding crazy.

I don't know this girl, and chances are I'll never see her again, so I decide to just go with it. "And anything about how to speak with ghosts." I'm waiting for a strange look or a judging expression, but she just grins and waves for me to follow her.

"Your best bet for anything related to ghosts will probably be the occult section. Here." We reach a row filled with books about witchcraft, demons, and ghosts, among other things.

"Uh, thanks." I'm not really sure where to start, and perhaps she senses it.

"So, you want something about talking with ghosts?" I nod.

Again, I'm waiting for a judgmental look, but she just sets down her pile and begins pulling books off the shelf and stacking them in my hands. She provides commentary about a few of the books too.

"I've read this one, it's a good sort of intro into the realm of the supernatural, and the author is a local." The book in question is titled *The Ghosts You Don't Know,* and it's got a colorful cover that belies its sinister topic. The author is Carren Roche... as in my *therapist*; I make a mental note to ask her about the book in our next session.

"This one talks a lot about rituals and stuff, but it might have something in it that you're looking for. This one is filled with personal anecdotes from mediums with stories about hauntings. It's more of a thrilling type of read. And this one features the personal history of a medium that works with the cops. This one is a general intro to Wiccan and this—"

"I don't think I need that one." I cut her off. If I didn't say something I think she'd send me home with every book in this row.

"These should do for now. Thanks!"

"Not a problem. Are you looking for anything else or would you like to go ahead and check those out?" She asks but doesn't wait for me to respond. "If you're interested we just updated our YA section. And I remember a few good books that feature ghosts." Her eagerness hangs in the air between us, and I can't bring myself to turn her down.

"Lead away."

Amongst the teen books she pulls a few that feature creepy looking houses and one that even has a pale looking girl standing amongst a cemetery. That one looks familiar for some reason and I'm wondering if I might have read it before. Regardless if I have or not, it sounds interesting enough.

"I think I like reading." I think aloud. The girl looks at me and giggles.

"I'd hope so... I mean you are in a library and all. So, is supernatural your favorite genre?" I laugh as well.

"I don't really know."

Now, there's the look I'd been waiting for. I start to go in my spiel about the amnesia and for the first time I feel a kind of relief. I don't know this person and she doesn't know me. It doesn't matter to her that I lost my memories, she won't be disappointed.

She expects nothing from me. What shocks me the most though, is that I don't get a pitying look from her. Instead she grins from ear to ear.

"Then I guess you get to start all over in the reading department. That's kind of cool to be able to reread books with a more open mind..." She catches herself, maybe realizing that she could be coming across as insensitive. "Umm... that is, it's just... well it sucks that you lost your memories and all... I don't mean to be so callous... but...." She trails off and I start laughing again.

"No, I get what you mean. It's nice to meet someone that can point out the bright side and all. And I think I was a reader. So, it might be interesting just to see if any memories come back." And I guess that's what does it.

It's like I opened a floodgate and the girl begins to ramble passionately about what books I should read first and which I should add for later.

By the time Cadence texts me to tell me he's outside, I've got a stack of books to last me awhile... unless I discover that I'm a fast reader or something, and that's not including my research books for Evan.

Who, of course, is sitting at a nearby table, head bowed down, with what looks like a book in front of him. If I wasn't worried about appearing crazy I'd go over just to see if the book is real or not.

"Oh, I didn't get your name?" I ask the girl as I'm heading out. She's not wearing a name tag or anything, though it's obvious she works here.

"Risa. It was great talking with you Lyric. Be sure to come back and let me know how you like my suggestions."

On the way home, I tell Cadence about the books and Risa, trying to casually find out if I used to be a reader or not.

"Strange, you never really were in to reading. You mainly just read what you had to for school. But if you're going to get into it now, then I got some great recommendations."

It's a little disheartening to find that I wasn't a reader, I really thought I was on to something and then another realization hits me.

"But I knew that there was a good selection of books there, and it all felt familiar."

"That's because I used to make you go there with me all the time after school. We'd walk around downtown and then go to the library, sometimes staying until they closed. Evan, Darryl, and Margaret often came with us. We'd do homework and study there on days we needed the quiet."

This is one of the first times Cadence has casually let slip about Evan and the others, Darryl and Margaret, that died in the crash.

I'm not sure why no one wants to talk about them, as if they're afraid of mentioning them, or maybe it hurts too much? I'm not ready to ask yet. Asking about Evan, who's still alive is one thing, but it feels wrong to ask about the couple that I don't remember.

Especially when I've been told that we were all close. I'm sure Cadence is suffering far more than he wants me to know. Instead of focusing on his grief he's focusing on me, but he's essentially lost all his best friends, even me, if you count the old me

"Oh... so you're a reader?" Cadence chuckles and I wonder if I used to tease him about being a bookworm. This is a side of him that he hasn't shown me yet. The focus is normally on me, so it's nice to learn more about him for once.

"Something like that. I want to be a writer or an editor. I'm not sure which. I just love books. I love reading and writing, and stories, anyone's stories, and I want to be a part of the process one day."

Cadence assails me with details of his favorite books and the novel he's been secretly working on. It sounds rather interesting, an epic fantasy series about a seer.

When we get home, I decide to read Carren's book first, but my bedroom light is flickering again. It's been flickering every now and then, pretty much since I came back from the hospital.

I've changed the light bulb a few times, but the flickering hasn't stop. Reid checked the wiring but found nothing wrong. We even got my eyes checked, thinking it was some after affect from my injury.

I'm just stuck with a flickering light. As if the light wasn't bad enough, when I look up from the book, Evan is sitting at the foot of my bed, a grin splitting his face.

"Seriously I wish you'd just tell me what you want already." Of course, it wouldn't be that easy. He doesn't respond but makes himself comfy. He's never been in my room before, so I take that as a sign that I'm on the right track.

Carren's book describes ghosts as lingering spirits that often have unfinished business. It really is a sort of intro guide to the supernatural... or as Carren refers to it, 'the spirit realm.' It's not cut and dry like I was expecting but filled with personal stories and anecdotes, not all of which are Carren's own stories, but I guess some of those she's helped.

"You have unfinished business? Why don't you just tell me what it is then." I say to Evan. His head tilts to the side and I find myself reaching forward to touch him. Before I can reach him, he gets up and disappears through my door. Yeah, like I really thought that would work.

I skip ahead in the book to the section about summoning and talking to spirits. I'm thinking the summoning part won't be too hard since I see Evan all the time... it's the getting him to talk to me that's my problem.

Though the book suggests never trying to contact the spirit realm on your own, something about it being dangerous, I really can't think of anyone that I would want to ask to help me. There's a few options that she provides but I rule most of them out. I'm not going to try to buy a spirit board for one use.

The séance seems pretty doable with a dowsing pendulum, though. And I remember seeing a crystal on my desk that could probably work for the pendulum. I settle on that and start making a list of the other things I need. Even though she stresses that it's not something a person should do on their own, especially a beginner, there's no one I want to ask.

I could probably get Carren herself to help, but she's my therapist and all, and that's got to be a breach of something. Plus, I don't want her knowing how crazy I really am. My second thought is asking Cadence, one of my other brothers, or even Risa for help. But I don't really want to involve Cadence or anyone from my family, and I don't know Risa well enough to ask her, so alone it is.

By the time Serenity calls me down for dinner I've got a rough plan to perform a séance, it's just a matter of getting the necessary equipment and when. But maybe then, Evan's ghost will talk to me.

Chapter 6

Mama Etta is just leaving when I reach Evan's hospital room. Her hair is a fiery orange today. "Oh dearie, two visits in one week, Evan will be pleased. I was just stepping out to get a bite to eat." She crushes me in a hug. "You need me to bring you anything dear?" I shake my head no and she gives me a pat on the head. "Now do remember to stop in for tea soon." She says with a wave as she hobbles off.

I'm greeted by the familiar site of Evan and the steady beeping of machines.

"I've decided how to help you." I say, wasting no time on formalities, not that I ever do anyway. I automatically reach for his curls again and begin braiding, wanting the comfort. I tell him all about looking up ghosts and Carren's book.

"She's the hippy therapist I told you about before. From what I read, I think maybe you have unfinished business. If you would just talk to me I could help you, but maybe you're scared? I just... I want to know what happened, you know. And it's weird... like I don't really know you," at least not anymore, "but I don't know how to put it... I feel," I look down at my hands curled through his hair.

"Comfortable, I feel really comfortable with you for some reason." As I say the words out loud it becomes so obvious I can't believe I hadn't realized it sooner. I'd already felt things were easy being with him.

My family told me about Evan pretty much as soon as I woke up. I've been visiting him since that first week and just never stopped. I don't know whether it's the fact that he's the only one that was there with me the night of the accident or whether there's something more to it, but I feel like I can breathe best when I'm with him.

"I wonder why... maybe, maybe because you can't talk back? You can't tell me about me. You have no expectations of me. You're the only one I really feel like I can be myself around, at least the me I am now."

But it's more than just easy, more than just a level of comfort, I like being around Evan. There's this sense of rightness, of familiarity that I dare not tell anyone. No, I don't know him anymore, maybe I never will again but...

"You... I want to help you. Even-even if I can't help myself, if anything, I want to help you move on... I *will* help you move on. I promise you." I lay a hand over his beating heart as I make the promise.

I don't know how I'll feel when I can't visit him anymore. I think I'll most likely be sad, but it'd be selfish to not do anything. It'll be for the best for him to move on.

"And Mama Etta, I'll go visit her as often as I can, so she's not lonely." I add.

Having said all that, I feel lighter, freer. I remember the other reason I'm here to talk with him and reach forward and pull a couple strands of his hair out, apologizing as I do so.

I need them for the séance. It said in the book to use something that would mean something to the spirit, or something that the spirit owned. And what better thing than some strands of his hair.

And then I sit for a while talking about random things: the weather, my dinner last night, Risa and the books she recommended. I talk with him until Mama Etta is back and then I say a quick goodbye, making promises to stop by soon, and head out.

Since it's a weekday I know Clef is somewhere around here. I decide to surprise him with a visit. I don't remember what floor he's usually on but since I'm well known as Clefs little amnesiac sister, and from my frequent visits to see Evan, it shouldn't be too hard to find him.

At the nearest nurse's station sits a redheaded woman who I've become decently acquainted with. She's about the same age as the twins and her name tag declares her a Bridget.

She's leaned forward in her chair, doodling on a pad of sticky notes as I approach. Everything about Bridget is round, from her roundish bob to round eyes framed by round glasses and even a rounded neckline. She's got a bubbly personality that suits her petite and round appearance. Her eyes light up and she smiles one of those full smiles with dimples when she sees me.

"Lyric! How are you doing?" Oh yes, the well-meaning double-edged question that everyone always asks. Sometimes it's a greeting but in my case, given my accident, what she's really asking is if I'm better. If I remember.

It would be perfectly acceptable if I told her how I really feel, but I don't. I don't want to talk about it. Bridget likes to talk, so I keep my answer succinct.

"Fine. Just fine. Do you know where Clef might be?" I keep my voice light and respectful, even throw in a smile for good measure, but I still catch a pitying look in her eyes. I hate those.

"Oh, I believe he's on his lunch break about now, try the cafeteria dear." She gives me a smile that thankfully erases the pity. Every smile she gives is always the same full smile, as if she really means it.

It's hard not to give a genuine smile in return. I tell her thanks and head for the cafeteria before she can sweep me into a conversation.

I'm not really that surprised that Bridget knows Clef's schedule. I've been coming here long enough to see the way she looks at him. Though it's obvious Clef barely knows of her. I'd attribute it to the fact that he recently broke up with someone he thought he'd marry, but really, I think he's just genuinely clueless.

Cadence told me it was Analise confessing that started their relationship, that prior to her confession Clef didn't pay any attention to her.

A girl that looks like a model going unnoticed to the point that she blurted out her feelings, I imagine it was hilarious.

That's part of why it was such a shock when he announced their engagement after only two months of dating, sure they'd been interning together but they barely knew one another.

I make a mental note to find a way to get Bridget and Clef to talk. Compared to Analise, she's a girl next door in looks, but she definitely is a whole lot nicer. And even though Clef has sworn off women, maybe getting him to befriend someone as bubbly as her could help him, even if they don't date.

"No, I've said it enough. I don't want to talk things out, I'm done listening to your ridiculous excuses. You've burned that bridge." I stop at the corner near the cafeteria entrance. That's Clef's voice.

"Please, just a few minutes. Do you not miss us? Do you not want to make things *right*?" I recognize the other voice as Analise.

"I'm done. I don't have to make anything right. I did nothing wrong. I shouldn't have given you a second chance the first time. You're so full of yourself. Go talk to the guy you cheated on me with." His voice sounds raw as if he's had to repeat himself too many times.

"Please, just go." His voice is lower now, these words almost a whisper.

It occurs to me that I shouldn't be eavesdropping, that there's still time to walk away or reveal myself but I stand transfixed. I wonder what sort of excuses she keeps making. What possible excuse could she think justifies her actions?

"Please, love? Just a few minutes, that is all I ask. Just talk to me. I miss talking to you." I can imagine this is accompanied by one of those arm pats, but I don't want to give myself away by peeking. "Come on, my love," the 'my love' bit is grating on my nerves.

They didn't even date for that long and she was cheating on him, but fancied herself in love?

"Please," Clef's voice sounds so small and pitiful, so empty. It's so different from at home. I think maybe a part of him did love her, or at least the idea of her, "just go."

There's so much defeat in that plea, as if he's given up, as if he knows she won't listen and it plucks at my heart. Before she can respond, I stumble forward.

"Clef! There you are, I've been looking everywhere. I came to have lunch with you." Both of them jump slightly as if I've startled them. I can see the relief in Clef's eyes at the same time I see the question. I bet he'll ask me later how much I heard.

Analise's eyes narrow and she purses her lips. She's angry I interrupted them. I can practically feel waves of irritation spilling off her. Her face gets a nasty twisted grimace before she quickly conceals it, giving Clef a side-glance, possibly to make sure he didn't see it. Did I really think her face beautiful?

64

Perhaps it's irritation, but she couldn't be uglier.

I give a grin, and plaster an innocent look on my face, then as if I'm noticing her for the first time, I widen my eyes a bit in her direction.

"Oh, am I interrupting something?" I ask. I turn to look at Clef, pointedly ignoring Analise.

His eyes twitch to her and he shakes his head. "No, nothing at all. I was just about to go eat." It's clear he doesn't want to introduce us and since he doesn't know we've met again, I play dumb.

"Oh, well nice meeting you, sorry I have to steal him away." I say with a passing glance at Analise. There's fire in her eyes. Clef strides forward and wraps me in a bear hug.

"Thanks for coming Leary. I'll treat you to some hot cocoa." Analise looks like she's about to say something, so I talk over her.

"With marshmallows and some pie?" I ask. Clef chuckles and nods. Apparently old me had just as bad of a sweet tooth as the me now, and I know the familiarity is probably reassuring to him.

"Sure, what kind of pie? I think there's chess, peach, coconut cream, and maybe some blueberry today."

Without a word of goodbye, we leave Analise standing alone in the hall. Neither of us even glances back.

"Hmmm, what kind of pie did I like before?" Clef's gaze shifts over me, I can see his shoulders visibly relaxing, his muscles unfurling as the tension leaves him. He smiles, a real smile that touches his eyes, making them crinkle around the corners. I rarely ask questions like this and he welcomes the distraction.

"Your favorites were key lime and lemon meringue. You said they made you think of the beach."

"Ah but since they don't have those, what's *your* favorite?" He pauses for a moment, looking deep in thought, but I don't think he's thinking of pie. "I bet its coconut cream, because you're always nutty." He lets out a startled laugh at my stupid joke.

"And you would be wrong my dear Leary. Next guess?"

"Hmmm... Chess because it rhymes with Clef?"

"That doesn't rhyme."

"Uh huh, it's a slant rhyme." I say, sticking my tongue out. "No go?" He shakes his head.

We get in line and he grabs a tray, placing three sandwiches and a couple bags of chips on it. We're nearing the dessert and I wonder if he's really wanting me to keep this guessing game going for the distraction, or if a part of him is hoping I might just remember something as insignificant as what kind of pie his favorite is. At this point it's getting to process of elimination, unless his favorite isn't one on the list of today's pies.

"Hmmm... is it one from the list you gave me?"

"That's cheating. You have to guess." He says as he places two fruit cups on the tray and starts filling a cup with coffee.

I think for a moment of what little I know about Clef's eating habits. I'm still having trouble with telling him and Alto apart but thankfully their eating habits are as similar as their faces.

Their sweet tooth's probably rival my own, or perhaps the whole family just has a sweet tooth, except Harp who likes to drink black coffee, black tea, and even eats oatmeal without any added sugar.

Alto and Clef always drink their coffee choked with cream and sugar, they like sugar in their grits, they drown their pancakes in blueberry syrup. They don't like strawberry or grape jam but will eat jars of... I know what it is.

"Blueberry, because you only eat blueberry jam, and you're always using blueberry syrup. And you love the homemade blueberry muffins that Serenity-Mom makes."

Clef looks genuinely surprised. He drops the coffee lid he's holding.

"I'm right aren't I?" I ask as he bends to retrieve the lid. His mouth gapes a bit.

"Did you?" I shake my head. I didn't remember that. I deduced it.

"Sorry... it was just a really good guess. I was thinking about your eating habits." No need to let him know I was thinking of *Alto's* and his eating habits, neither of them need to know that I can't tell them apart most of the time, that'd only hurt their feelings.

"It's..." He sighs and reaches for two packets of hot chocolate. "It's okay Leary, that was good guesswork." He gives me a grin over the steaming water pouring into the powdered cocoa. "Two slices of blueberry pie it is."

When the cup is halfway full he pours in vanilla and caramel creamer. I arch a brow as he passes the cup to me along with a little stirrer. "Believe me, you love it this way. Makes it's creamier."

I stir silently as we make our way to the pies, two plates of blueberry pie are placed on the crowded tray and then to a cooler of little mini servings of ice-cream, chocolate and vanilla find their ways to the tray, and then he pays for everything and we take our seats. He's right about the hot chocolate, it is creamier.

"Not bad for hospital food." I say, digging into the pie first, even though he hands me one of the sandwiches, it appears to have some unidentifiable lunch meat with lettuce and tomato on it.

The label says turkey, didn't know turkey came in that shade, I'm rethinking my earlier statement. Clef catches the look I give the turkey sandwich.

"You think this is bad then you should see what we feed the patients. Let's just say, you're lucky we were bringing you food before you were released."

He scarf's down both his sandwiches before I'm even three bites into my pie. "This is restaurant quality compared to that stuff." He says around a mouth full of food.

We eat in silence for a bit and then when he's done with his chips and inhaling the fruit cup he looks up at me and lets out another sigh.

"That girl you saw in the hall..." He lets it hang, as if waiting for my permission to tell me. My acting must've been pretty good if he didn't catch on that I knew her. I almost say I know but I don't want surprise him into thinking I remembered, and then have to tell him the truth. So, I widen my eyes and play dumb again.

"What about her?" He's mangling a bit of pear with his fork, but I can tell he wants to say it, perhaps he needs to.

"She's my ex." He lets the last word hang for a bit and I can tell it's a conscious decision not to add fiancée.

I let my mouth form a little O of surprise.

"You heard... didn't you?" Busted. I nod... now this... I don't want to lie about.

"We broke up a little after your accident," before I can respond he rushes to explain that it had nothing to do with me and everything to do with her being a cheater.

"She was fooling around with someone before she even asked me out and when she asked me out... they didn't stop. I caught them in a janitor's closet. He was the janitor." The way he says the story, as if he's listing groceries that we need, no emotion at all, it's clear he's said the words many times before.

"Should I go back and pull her hair out for you? We could make a wig out of it." My response must catch him off guard because for a moment his mask slips and I can see the pain and betrayal he's still feeling.

"You know... that's exactly something the old you would say." He digs into his pie as way of ending the talk of Analise and I decide to change the subject.

"Tell me about your internship?" I say, and Clef jumps at the topic. Telling me about how he decided to go into the medical field after his appendix burst.

"I was your age when it happened, you know." He glances down at his melting ice cream.

"They... the doctors that is, they were just so awesome. I mean I'd been to the hospital before, but I'd never had to have a surgery, and everything was so fast. I was terrified, but I realized I wanted to be like them, to be able to fix things... and to save people like that."

He talks about how he focused even more on his studies after that and graduated high school a year early. He lights up as he talks, and I can tell he really loves what he's doing.

* * *

When I get home I'm exhausted, but I feel content, like I've accomplished more than I really have. I lay back in my bed listing the things I still need for the séance and twirling Evan's hair around my fingers.

Chapter 6

My bedroom light flickers again. It's always flickering. No one else notices but me and nothing we've done so far has made it go away.

Frustrated, I go to the utility closet and grab the box of bulbs again. Since I have nothing better to do, I fully intend on replacing it again and again until I find a bulb that doesn't flicker.

The box is empty, and I reach farther in the closet to the box behind it, making a mental note to tell Reid and Serenity that the bulbs are nearly out. The box is a little heavier than bulbs usually are. When I get it to the light of the hallway I see it's not a box of bulbs at all. It's got a book in it, the cover is soft yellow leather and the pages have uneven edges, there's a little clasp in the front with a lock on it. My initials are engraved on the cover.

"Well, it looks like I found my missing journal." I say aloud, peering at Godzilla who's leaned against the wall watching me. When I'm back in my room... the light has stopped flickering.

Chapter 7

"Where would I hide a key?" I ask Cadence. That question had seemed like such an easy one five days ago, but after tearing apart my bedroom and searching all sorts of hiding places in the house, I still haven't found it.

"Key for what?" He asks, pausing his computer game. I hold the yellow journal up and tap the lock. It's not one of those typical diary locks that any sort of skeleton key could open, but a custom lock. He glances at the book for a moment and then his eyes widen, and he jumps up.

Perdita, who was lounging at his feet, walks off with a twitch of her tail, showing her displeasure at being disturbed.

"You found it?" He asks, eyes darting from me to the book.

"Yeah, it was in the utility closet in a light bulb box, weird right?" He chuckles, sitting back down in his seat.

"Yup, sounds exactly like you. I think you hid it in a new place every week too. I read it *once*, and you never trusted any of us after that. Even though that was when you were like ten."

"So, any ideas of where I hid the key?" Cadence sits pondering for a moment.

"Well, where all have you looked?" He asks.

He opens up a Word document and begins listing the places as I say them. The first day I'd checked all over my room, tearing clothes from my closet and rifling through my cluttered desk.

When I came up empty I searched all through the house, back to the utility closet, in the kitchen and living room, even the little bowl where spare keys were kept by the door, that one was a long shot.

The cats must've thought I was crazy because I even looked in their cat tree. I also looked in Godzilla's giant dog bed that he only uses when we're in the living room. When I'm finished Cadence muses over the list before swiveling his chair around and leaping up.

"So basically, you've only looked in the obvious places." He says walking out of the room with me at his heels.

"I'll have you know I even checked inside the fridge and kitchen cabinets, and under the litterboxes." He's laughing again.

"Yeah, but you looked in plain sight, didn't you? Except maybe under the litterboxes, that's a rather unique place. I take it you didn't find anything?"

"Actually, there was a plastic bag with a wad of money in an envelope labeled L's Emergency Fund."

"Seriously?" Cadence laughs when I pull the envelope out of my pocket.

"I counted it, there's two hundred and fifty dollars in here."

"You were always saving your birthday money, I wouldn't be surprised if you had a few more stashes of cash hidden in the house. So, aside from that... you have to realize that you..." He trails off to look at me, I can see concern knitting his eyebrows. He's probably worried he'll offend me.

"Don't stop, tell me." He nods. We come to my bedroom and he crosses over to my mussed-up desk.

"You were obsessed with detective stuff, murder mysteries. You said you wanted to be a spy when we were little." He holds up the magnifying glass off my desk and holds it in front of one of his eyes.

"You never read any mysteries, but you watched them all the time," he looks thoughtful a moment. "Well, now that you're reading I've got some great murder mysteries you might like, but anyway the point is you would never have hidden anything in plain sight or in the obvious places, but knowing you, you would've kept it somewhere in your room."

"But by that description doesn't the desk seem like the most unlikely choice." Cadence gives a noncommittal shrug and begins pulling the drawers out of my desk.

He sets them on the bed and then pulls up a flashlight app on his phone to look at the inside of the desk. I hadn't even thought of pulling the drawers out, he crawls out from under the desk and passes the flashlight on the underside of the attached table. He stands back up.

"Well, that didn't work... uh maybe try looking at the back of your pictures?" I move around the room as he starts putting the drawers back. But no key. We begin moving around the room checking hiding spots I hadn't thought to look at before.

Godzilla, laying in front of my door like normal, gets up and walks away, as if our movements are disturbing him.

Cadence looks under my rug and I move to my bookshelf, it's filled with mainly DVDs and CDs, but I start rifling through the few books, even though I did that on day three. I open up each DVD and CD, seeing if there's anything in the cases besides what's supposed to be there. After about 15 minutes, and surprisingly finding twenty dollars hidden with the movie *Dracula*, my room is even more of a disaster than before.

"I was pretty good at hiding things, wasn't I?"

Cadence flops down on my bed and begins tossing a stuffed bumblebee up and down in the air.

"Yeah, we never could find any Christmas gifts you hid. Mom and Dad made you officially in charge of hiding them when you turned six. Something about you being the only one that they could trust not to open them." I laugh.

"I was a good kid." Cadence rolls up to look at me.

"You still are." He bounces up. "Come on, there has to be another place to look." I shake my head and sit at my desk, swiveling back and forth in my chair. My eyes cut back to the drawers.

"I think it's probably gone for good... or wait a minute." We'd thought to look behind the drawers, but... I start pulling the drawers out of the desk again.

"Already did that Leary." I turn the drawers over dumping out the contents in a heap as I look at the bottoms of the drawers. I gesture to one of them and Cadence follows my lead. I turn it over and then upon seeing nothing on the underside, flip it back and begin running my hands over the bottom of the wood.

"Look for indents or something... maybe I thought to make a false bottom? And don't forget to turn it over and look underneath." There's nothing, though, and Cadence turns up nothing as well. I lean back against my desk eying the mess of rolling pens, rubber bands, and scraps of paper surrounding me.

One piece catches my eye, with *A Midsummer Night's Dream* on the top and a list of audition times along with the address of The Rising Eclipse Theater. I'd circled one of them.

"Check this out." I gesture to Cadence, pointing at the paper. "I mean I was told I auditioned and everything but it's one thing to be told, and then to see the proof."

"Hmm, I remember that day. You and Evan made up this really lame excuse as to why you needed to borrow the car, but no one even questioned it. I mean, it was an obvious lie, something about needing to go and buy sunscreen."

Cadence gets a faraway look in his eyes, staring at the drawer in his hands.

"When the two of you had a treasure hunt, or were trying to find ghosts, or were chasing one of your mysteries you would sometimes get all secretive like that. You both liked telling the story at the end, so everyone could be surprised. I just assumed it was another one of your adventures."

I make a mental note to ask more about that later and turn to take in more of my demolished room. There's piles of clothes everywhere and my rugs and pillows are in heaps, stacks of books, CDs, and DVD's litter the floor. Hopefully, I can convince Cadence to help me clean.

Cadence flops down on the floor. Godzilla musters up the courage to come in the room and lays his large body beside him, putting his head on Cadence's chest and nudging at him until he starts scratching behind his ears.

"Seriously, you are way too good at this. You might want to consider a career in witness protection." I lay back too, closing my eyes and trying to think of hiding places.

"I think I might just need to give up on this."

"No... finding the key to your journal could be good for you. It's one thing to hear stories about yourself from us... but to read them in your own writing, maybe that could jog your..." He trails off. "Sorry."

"No need to apologize... I was thinking the same thing." I sit up and grab one of the escaping pens and a pad of paper and begin listing the places I've looked. "Logically there has to be some sort of solution. You're sure it would be hidden in my room, right?" Cadence nods. "Ok, so we've already ruled all the obvious and a few of the not as obvious places..."

I take in the furniture in the room. A twin bed, bookshelf, two nightstands, and a dresser. I don't really feel like checking all the other drawers, and I can see Cadence eying them with a resigned expression.

"So, before we tear all the drawers out let's rationalize this. I doubt I would've hid a key anywhere not easily accessible, and if I kept it in here, it would probably be near the bed and desk, which are the most likely places to write."

Cadence moves to check one of the nightstands and I check the other. After that turns up nothing, I scan my messy room again.

This is getting old but it's impossible to stop now. I've been obsessing over the location of this key for days, and this is perhaps the closest I've felt to finding it.

Now would be the perfect time for Evan to show up and help me. And that's the other thing, I've been so distracted with finding the key that I haven't had time to complete my séance, and I haven't seen Evan since the last time he was in my room.

My eyes dart back to my desk sliding over the assortment of notebooks, pencil cups, pictures, the little calendar with puppies on it that's two years old, and a cute little tape dispenser that looks like a cat. Every bit of it I've already checked, my eyes slip to the empty space where the drawers are supposed to be.

Logically I know it's not there, but for some reason I keep getting a nagging feeling that I'm missing something. Cadence plops down on my desk chair and starts swiveling around.

"Oh my gosh! Cadence you're a genius!" I say as it hits me.

I know where the key is.

"Get up now!" Cadence is gaping at me but allows me to push him from the chair. I turn it over to look at the bottom of it. Cadence hovers behind me, practically bouncing on his feet. Even Godzilla moves closer to peer beside us. We let out twin sighs of content.

"I think you're probably the brilliant one. Who would've ever suspected the bottom of a chair." Cadence says as I pull the taped key off the chair, a grin splitting my face. It took five days and my room looks like a toddler's playroom, but I found it.

As if he knew I was one-step closer to possibly remembering him, I see Evan hovering by the door with a beautiful smile in my direction.

Chapter 7

Cadence leaves me to read my journal. He's practically buzzing with the same excitement that I have.

"Should I start from the beginning?" I ask Evan, who's sitting at my desk now, I almost expect the chair to start spinning but nothing moves. And as usual, he doesn't respond.

The first entry is dated almost two years ago, starting at the start of my freshman year of high school. I'm relieved to see that it's not coded, I'd hate to have to search for a key to decipher it, but there are abbreviations throughout it that make some stuff hard to understand.

Also, I never refer to anyone by their actual name, but by nickname and some by the first letters of their names. The first few entries are mindless babble talking about my day, TV shows, school. I find mention of acting a few times but never more than a few sentences here and there and nothing to say I actually had any roles or anything.

A lot of entries involve a person named Curls that I assume is Evan. Some talk about just going to different places, the movies, beach, rock climbing, sometimes different museums. Taking our dogs for hikes or walks in the park. There's even mention of ziplining and white water rafting a few times. I think we might've been adrenaline junkies.

Cadence wasn't kidding about the treasure hunting and other adventures either. We went to a lot of haunted houses and followed any myth, lore, or historical story that mentioned treasure. I don't read all of the entries, wanting

80

to go back and pay more attention to them later, but there's a lot of them.

I skip forward until I find mention of a few visits to the community theater and improv classes we were secretly attending.

"I wonder what the secrecy was for." I tell Evan.

There's also a lot of mention of a C and Rip. After a few more entries I'm pretty certain C is Cadence and Rip is Darryl. Mainly from the amount of time I spent with the two. The entries range from trivial day to day things to all sorts of fun things the four of us did. We especially liked hiking and rock climbing and we'd tried surfing a few times on Darryl's insistence, but Evan and I hadn't been very good at it.

Near the end of the year there's mention of Darryl meeting someone titled the Python. I really didn't like her. Citing the reason that she was too girly, clingy, and vain. I skip forward to earlier this year until I find an entry of a Viper sinking its fangs into Thing 1. I'm assuming that's one of the twins and with the way I trash the Viper, I think she's probably Analise.

Cadence wasn't kidding that I didn't like her, but he wasn't lying when he said I was close to her. I thought myself a sort of double agent. I started hanging out with her all the time, trying to convince her to tell me her secrets.

I secretly thought she was vapid and narcissistic and was trying to sabotage the relationship. We had nothing in common and from what I could tell, she had little in common with Clef too.

'*Went out for coffee and shopping with Viper. Saw her checking out other guys but she didn't confess anything, standby. She tried to give me relationship advice too, like I'm really going to listen to her. She's far too clingy, what's worse Thing 1 is wrapped around her tail. Can't believe he's being so stupid.*

I feel gross just hanging out with her. Must detox Thing 1 immediately, before things get worse.'

I continue reading, searching the entries in the hope of any clues, trying to read dual meanings in every word.

"I really was cautious." I tell Evan. I've gotten so used to talking to him now, that I do it without thinking. "I hid my journal, hid the key to it, and still didn't even write much that would even be worth hunting it down. I don't get it. Why all the secrecy for something so dull?" And I was also starting to wonder about my personality.

Everyone described me as optimistic and outgoing, but no one mentioned that I was a little judgmental, then again maybe I didn't let anyone on to that. Maybe I saved those thoughts for here. I wonder if Cadence knew.

There's a few more entries of the Python. She and Darryl had started dating and I was still unhappy with having her around.

' *Went out to movies with C, Curls, Rip and the Python. Don't know why Rip likes Python so much. She's sooooo annoying but the movie was good even if Rip and Python were making out the entire time. Ditched the lovebirds after the movie and went out for ice cream with Curls and C was being lame and bailed. I think he's hiding something, but he keeps dodging my questions. If he's hiding a gf then we're going to fight.'*

"Well, I think the Python is Margaret and I didn't like her." I didn't think she was bad like Analise, I just hadn't gotten to know her well.

'Rip and I got into it today. He gave me an ultimatum and I apologized to the Python. I was out of line. I'll admit she's trying hard, she isn't as bad as Viper, but I really don't see that we have anything in common.

Still don't get why Rip likes her. We've agreed to spend a day just the two of us. Rip really wants us to be friends. Curls didn't take my side. He said he just wants everyone to get along. C is still hiding something. I've ruled out a gf at least.'

"You're as bad as Clef. Just enamored with a pretty face." My voice echoes around the room. I hadn't heard it in awhile

"You're out of line this time. You're so certain that you won't like her that you haven't even given her a chance." This is one of the male voices that I remember hearing in the hospital.

I start skipping through the entries until I get to the day I spent with Margaret.

*'Surprisingly had a great time with Python...
M, she's not as vain as I thought. I'll give her
that. Not sure how I feel about her now, but I
did find out we have a few things in common.*

*I was rather shocked that she had us go on
an adventure by taking an old map of the city
and comparing how the landmarks had
changed. I thought Rip had put her up to it,
but she seemed genuinely interested in the
history of everything.'*

The next few entries are rather boring until
I get to one mentioning the Viper again.

*'Viper has convinced Thing 1 to tie the
knot. She's poisoned everyone but me and
Mom. We'll stop this. I think I know what
she's hiding now, just have to prove it. Thing
1 won't listen without proper evidence.'*

So, I thought I knew her secret... but I
wonder if I got the chance to confront her or
not? I wonder if the secret was that she'd been
cheating as the whole family now knew.
Maybe the plan had been something to get
Clef to catch her in the act?

*'Met up with Viper again over coffee. I'll be
putting my plan in action tomorrow. Plan on
surprising her at work and letting Thing 1 see
her fangs.'*

The next entry is scribbled furiously.

*'Didn't work, must reconvene. If it comes
down to it, I may need to confront that snake.
Curls, Rip, and C all think it's a bad idea. C is
mad because I didn't tell him about my plan,
but he's still hiding something and been all
brooding lately and he can't act as well as Curls*

*and I. I will not allow Viper to poison Thing 1
any more than she already has. M is on my
side at least. I'm really starting to like this girl.'*

"Well, it looks like Margaret and I did
finally start to bond. That's good to know." I
skip through a few more entries. They're just
blurbs about school and trying to figure out a
better way to prove that Analise is cheating
amongst a bunch of whining that Cadence was
hiding something.

"We hung out a lot." I add to Evan, who
strangely enough looks as if he's fallen asleep
at my desk. Can ghosts sleep?

*' Went to park with Curls to walk his Shakes
and GZ. Lots of fun. Granny sent us a picnic
to eat. That woman sure can cook. She even
made blueberry scones, had to save a few for
Things 1 & 2. But bigger news, tomorrow the
troop is going to investigate.*

*C backed out but I'm sure he'll join
eventually, he hates to be left out, still need to
talk about what he's hiding. I think it's about
college, but he's only a junior. Don't know
why he won't tell me. Mom think he's worried
I won't like whatever it is. Only consolation is
that he hasn't told the rents either.'*

That entry is dated just a month before the
accident. "The troop... so maybe our group of
friends?" I glance over at Evan who is asleep.
I wonder if that book on ghosts would tell me
whether ghosts sleep or not.

I make a mental note of it as I read on. The
next few entries mention not finding much
during the investigation but say nothing as to

what we were investigating. There were two
things we were looking into and one of them
was supposedly time sensitive.

"I can only surmise that these investigations
had nothing to do with either Analise or
Cadence... nothing else." I say aloud to Evan.

I get to a part that talks about another plan
with the viper and how Margaret was helping
me but nothing about what happened.

I read more and more but the words are
starting to run together, and I keep blinking
back sleep. The closer I get to the accident,
the less the entries make sense. Words start to
blur as I continue reading and the next thing I
know Serenity is knocking on my door, telling
me to come down for dinner. I'm reeling
inwardly from a strange nightmare of being
chased by a giant machine and she seems to
notice but instead comments on the journal.

"You found your journal, I see." She says
with a small smile. I nod and follow her
downstairs, trying to shake off the last dregs of
my nightmare. Finding my journal has only
supplied me with more mysteries, but there's
one thing that I'm starting to see clearly, and
that is that I need to find out more details
about my accident.

Up until this point I've been pretty passive,
thinking that my memories would eventually
return like normal and I wouldn't have to
worry about it, wouldn't need to know the gory
details.

I never even asked much about the accident,
and from what I can tell, my family doesn't

know much anyway, but the entries in my journal are pointing to one clear thing. Whatever we were investigating probably had something to do with our accident.

Chapter 8

I light three white pillar candles that I found at the dollar store around a circle of salt. It's a full moon and it just seems like the right time to perform a séance. According to Carren the candles are supposed to help attract the spirits and set the mood.

The salt is supposed to cleanse the area of negativity. Carren also said to use sage, but I think the salt will probably be enough. I turn the overhead light off and place a bowl of Evan's favorite snack in the salt circle along with his hair. Trying to subtly figure out what he liked from Cadence was actually far easier than I thought it would be.

I sit cross-legged in front of the candles and pull out the pinkish crystal that was on my desk. I asked Cadence about it, and apparently, I collect rocks. There were a few other gemstones in a box in my bookshelf too, but the crystal must've been my favorite. Cadence said it was what started the collection.

It was a gift from Evan. So, that makes it even more perfect to use as a pendant since Carren said it's best to use something that has sentimental value for a pendant. I've tied a cord to the top of it to make it easy to swing, now comes the tricky part. Hopefully I'll do this right and Evan will finally talk to me.

I start with the self-meditation that Carren recommended, emptying my mind and stating my goals. Eyes still closed I focus on my breathing for a few minutes. And then I go through each muscle, tensing and slowly loosening them. When my entire body feels relaxed I start the invitation that Carren suggested using.

"Evan, I bring you offerings from life into death and invite you here. Please accept these gifts and commune with me. You are welcome here, Evan."

When I open my eyes I'm not surprised to see Evan sitting on the other side of the salt circle.

I have a piece of paper with yes and no written on it in front of me and I fumble with the crystal as I hold it over the paper. There's probably supposed to be more ceremony to this, but the book didn't specify much about how to start asking questions. It just said that once you have a response from the spirit to begin your questions. Appearing seems like a good enough response to me.

"Evan, are you stuck here, do you have unfinished business?" I ask.

I hold the pendant over the paper, waiting to see if it'll move. I think this is probably an obvious yes, but it'll help break the ice while I think of other things to ask. I mentally kick myself for not writing a list down.

As if he hears me, he tilts his head to the side and smiles but he doesn't speak, and the pendant doesn't swing.

"Do you need my help with anything?" I ask. My heartbeat is the only sound in the room. My fingers start cramping and I realize I'm holding the cord so tight it's left an indent in my palm. Still the pendant doesn't move. Evan just stares at me as if I should already know the answer.

"Are you going to wake up soon?" I ask. It's a long shot, but maybe he can answer this one.

"Can I help you?" I ask, quietly. No response. Just more staring.

There's a scratching at the door and I practically drop the pendant.

Godzilla, I forgot he doesn't like it when I leave the door all the way shut. He lets out a heartfelt awoooo and scratches again.

My nearly dropping the crystal must break this weird staring contest we have, because Evan gets up and simply disappears.

A little disheartened, I blow out the candles and get up to open the door for Godzilla who gives me tons of kisses and then makes himself comfy on my bed. He rolls around onto his back and gives me a mournful look until I give him belly scratches.

So, the séance didn't work, I think, as I clean up the salt from the floor and start putting everything away. I guess on to my next plan. I just have to get Cadence to agree to it.

* * *

"No." Cadence says, an irritated look on his face. My next step toward figuring out how to help Evan is to figure out what happened.

And the first step towards that would be to find out why I was there in the first place. So, my bright idea is to go to the scene of the accident, maybe see if seeing the place where I lost my memories would bring them back.

It's such a simple solution, I can't believe I didn't think of it sooner. Perhaps something in the area could jog my memory.

"Cadence, it's a logical—"

"Absolutely not. You should be focusing on getting better, not-not traipsing about at the place that..." He trails off, perhaps at a lack of an adjective that is negative enough to describe how he feels about said place.

"That's what I'm doing! I want to get better, I do, and I think that it might bring back some of my memories." Cadence is shaking his head vehemently. He stares down into his cup of frozen yogurt.

He's been stirring it since I asked him about stopping at the place where I had my accident, and it's now a cup of melty goo with bits of mangled strawberries and blueberries. He pushes the cup away and gives me a look that can only be described as pouty. "I thought maybe we could stop by after we finish here." I say.

"I doubt you'll remember anything from there."

He doesn't say what he's most likely thinking. He thinks I won't be able to handle it, that if I remember anything, it'll be the accident and that the trauma will stem any progress I've made, but he and I both know that I've made no progress.

While misguided, I can almost understand his reluctance, that he thinks he's protecting me from myself, but if anything, the place won't jog any memories anyway. And perhaps the old Lyric was so breakable, but *I* am not.

"It's worth a try, isn't it?" I reach across the Formica table and grab his hand. "Don't you think I'd like to remember everything? I'm a walking blank canvas. I can barely tell Clef and Alto apart, I don't know anything about you or Harp or Serenity and Reid, and that's another thing, it feels so weird calling people that I can't remember Mom and Dad that I haven't been able to say it. I have to remind myself of my own name."

I take a big breath of air, feeling a lot like a balloon about to deflate.

"All of you are strangers Cadence, we tried everything everyone else's way, why don't we try mine?" I ask.

Cadence sits back and blinks at me. I've said too much, I know. I wish I could snatch the words back, but they hang in the air between us, heavy and solemn.

"Never mind... why-why don't we go see a movie or something?" I say, suddenly wanting to backtrack. "You said something about a movie with pirates, and if I remember correctly we love pirates, so let's—"

"No." Cadence says, his eyes are shiny, as if he's about to cry. "No, you're right. You sat through hours of us telling you who you are, you didn't complain when we took you to practically every place you'd ever liked. I wasn't thinking about... you really can't tell Clef and Alto apart?" He asks

"Is that really relevant? They're identical." Cadence is laughing.

"No, it's just... when we were kids they used to trade places all the time and try to trick us, and you could always tell. They're voices are a little different, but you didn't even need to hear them to know. They'd just walk in the room, and little five-year-old you would just look at them and say, 'Why is Thing 1 wearing Thing 2's clothes?' And then we'd all laugh."

"I called them Thing 1 and Thing 2?"

"Oh yeah, it was their nicknames because they dressed as Thing 1 and 2 for Halloween one year and you never stopped calling them that." Cadence sits forward, his brows knit together. "Lyric, we'll go. I'll take you." I think my face might break, I'm grinning so big.

Not more than twenty minutes later Cadence pulls to the side of the road near a construction site. The bare bones of a building shooting from the earth enclosed by a chain link fence, yellow caution signs warn trespassers away, threatening fines and jail time. Piles of stone and dirt are spread out amongst machinery with tarps covering a few things here and there.

"This is it?" I ask looking around. "Was I in the construction site?" Cadence shakes his head, he's watching me far too intently.

"No."

I follow him on up the road where it begins to climb steadily uphill, there's a drop on one side, not very steep but enough to do damage. "The car was found down there." Cadence sits down in the gravel that litters the side of the road and kicks a rock down the incline.

"No one but me even knew you weren't home..." This is news to me.

"You knew?" Cadence gives me a tortured look.

"I was supposed to go with you. I had a paper to finish. I bailed and-and, you said you'd be back before midnight, and to cover for you. But then you weren't back, and you wouldn't answer your phone and... I should've been there." His guilt is tangible, like a spider web clinging to skin. I wonder if he's been hiding it this whole time.

"No, if you had been...." I don't say it, but he knows what I'm referring to. If he'd been there, he might've died too. I'm the lucky one that survived, that managed to walk away. "Do you know why we were here?" I ask. Cadence gives a dry laugh.

"I don't know all the details, you wouldn't tell me everything because I kept bailing on you during your investigation or whatever it was. Heck, all of you were a little irritated with me, even Evan, and I've seen him apologize to a wall for bumping into it," he lets out another laugh, this one a little lighter.

"A wall?"

"Well, he was tired and thought it was a person, but anyway I know it all started with something to do with Darryl and whatever it was, you said it was something big."

"Well, that is *so* not helpful." I sit down next to him and look out into the trees lining the roadside.

"Soooo... remember anything?" Cadence asks. I can tell by the way he asks that he knows I haven't. I shake my head. I stand and dust the gravel dust off my pants and walk toward the railing, it's not even dented or scratched.

"It's weird, the railing, that is. Did they repair it that fast? How'd they make it so seamless?" I ask, ignoring Cadence's question.

"No... they said that somehow the impact sent you flying right over the railing, it didn't need repairing."

Musing over this bit of information I glance down to the bottom of the drop, but nothing comes back to me, only a sense of vertigo.

It's just a normal roadside, just some dirt and trees. I don't even see Evan. I close my eyes and try to imagine what happened.

That's when I hear a scream, the sound of crunching metal.

"I love you guys. If this is how we go, I'm okay with that. If any of us makes it—"

Cadence taps me on the shoulder and the words fade away. It was a male voice, the same I heard in my room. I think it might be Darryl's.

"Anything?" Cadence asks. I shrug.

"I guess you were right, let's go."

The car ride is silent, I can practically feel his disappointment, but I don't really want to tell him about the voices, and it's not like it's a memory anyway. Maybe I'm hearing the ghost Darryl? But the fact that I hear my own voice doesn't make any sense and why do I only see Evan's ghost and not Margaret's and Darryl's?

To try and lighten the mood I convince him to stop by the library.

"Why did you want to come here?"

"I've got some returns to make." I pull the books out of my bag. "And you love it here." I say with a grin. Cadence rolls his eyes but from the smile on his face, he's happy for the distraction.

After turning the books in, I'm happy to find Risa in the aisles. Cadence is trailing behind me like a duckling.

"How'd you like those books?" Risa asks, casting a glance towards Cadence.

"Not bad, turns out I'm not as much a reader as I thought. He is though. Risa, my brother Cadence, Cadence, this is Risa." I say, because I can tell Cadence is waiting for introductions. Mainly by the not so subtle way he elbows me in the back.

"Wait, so you're Lyric and his name is Cadence. That's awesome!" Risa comments, and then with full attention on Cadence. "Nice to meet you." She offers her hand for him to shake. Cadence gives me a side glance as if he's never had to shake someone's hand before.

"We get that a lot," Cadence says. "Our brothers are also musical terms." Risa arches an eyebrow, "Clef, Alto, and Harp." Risa grins again.

"So, I take it your parents are in the music biz?" Cadence nods, explaining about how our parents during a performance in college. Serenity was in musical theater, Reid was in the orchestra. It's my first time hearing the story too.

"Well, before Cadence here tells you our entire life story, does the library have any newspaper archives?" Risa nods and motions me to follow her.

"Newspapers?" Cadence asks. I forgot to clue him in on my newest idea.

"I want to read up on all the details of the accident."

"All our newspapers are going to be in our online database," Risa says as she leads us to a set of ancient looking desktop computers. "They're a little slow, but they get the job done." Risa adds when she sees the look on my face.

"I think I'll go find something to read." Cadence says before leaving us. Risa shows me how to access the newspapers and how to use the search engine to find what I'm looking for and then leaves me alone. I start on the day of the accident, but there's nothing that I can find.

I find a small blurb about the car wreck the next day, it just talks about three critically injured in a severe car crash, one dying on impact, but mentions no names. From the description of the location, I know it's about us.

So, three of us made it to the hospital. I didn't know that. The next thing I find about the accident mentions the death of one of the car crash victims, another still in critical care, but the third was in stable condition. The third one must have been me.

I scour the next few days of information trying to find out anything I can, but the only other mention I find is about a memorial service for the two others that were in the car with us, held by what I assume is our high school.

Underneath a black and white photo of a football field full of students holding candles it says, 'Tonight the students of South Shores High School say farewell to fellow students, Margaret Elizabeth Aston and Darryl Johnson Davies with a candlelight vigil.'

The next pictures are school photos of the two. The girl has long straight hair and one of those faces that could be in magazines. She's got a secretive little smirk that indicates a sense of humor.

The boy is just as attractive. He has a piercing in one ear and a mischievous grin, he's got an eyebrow arched in the photo, as if he has a secret he's hiding from the camera.

I feel a tightening in my chest, I knew these people, and it feels so wrong that I can't even remember them. That nothing comes to mind when seeing their faces.

The article mentions that Margaret was an award-winning gymnast and Darryl was in the theater club. He was slated to play the cowardly lion in the end of year production of *Wizard of Oz*. Both were straight A students, well liked among the school.

The article includes a bit about their families. Darryl was being raised by his widowed mother. His father was a decorated soldier that died in the line of duty. Margaret had her parents that ran a successful furniture store and a little sister.

The article goes on to talk a little about their goals and includes a few quotes from students and family members, but none of it tells me about why all of us were out so late near a construction site. I decide to give up, just as Risa is coming back.

"You find what you were looking for?" She asks. I shake my head and suddenly find myself blurting out what I was trying to find.

"O-oh... well the best way to know is maybe to talk with their parents?" She suggests.

"Right, I didn't tell mine, but maybe one of them mentioned it to theirs." I thank her and go to hunt down Cadence.

When I find him, I stop for a moment to laugh. He's sitting on the floor amongst a pile of books, a worn pair of reading glasses sitting on top of his nose.

"Aren't those for old people?" I ask as I get closer. He jumps up, knocking over a few of the books.

"Maybe I'm old on the inside?" He says as he takes the glasses off and I watch as they fold all the way in half, and he sticks them in his pocket.

"Find anything?" He asks as he begins stacking the books into a single pile.

"No, but what can you tell me about Darryl and Margaret?" I ask.

Cadence casts a glance my way as he picks up his tall stack of books, supporting them with his chin. I reach over and grab a few before they topple off. He hides the surprise well, but I can see that the question shocks him a little. I hadn't asked about them.

Of course, they were mentioned just as much as Evan, but Evan felt so much more real and I feel a little guilty that I didn't ask about the pair sooner.

"There's not much to say. We were all friends. Best friends, really. I know you've been reading your journal, so chances are you probably wrote about hanging out all the time." A few more books almost topple down and I reach to grab them.

"We had movie nights once every week and most days we took turns studying at each other's houses. We've known Darryl for years. We both met him separately, he was in your year, but he became a big part of our family, just like Evan. The four of us, we did practically everything together."

Cadence swipes at his eyes a little and I pull him in for a hug, causing our book piles to wobble precariously.

"Darryl was a great guy. He was a jokester."

"And Margaret?" I ask. I know from my journal that I hadn't been fond of her at first, but I want to know what Cadence thought of her.

"We hadn't known Margaret for long. He'd been talking to her for maybe a few months before he officially introduced us all and they hadn't been dating long, maybe three or four months."

"What were they both like?"

"Darryl was a goof. He was always making up jokes, often at his own expense. He was amazing at impressions, and he was always constantly playing pranks and devising new ways to get us to laugh. He used to help us play pranks on the twins and dad."

"We played pranks on them?"

"Oh yeah, there's an ongoing prank war in the house. I'm actually surprised they've held off this long on pulling one." Cadence gives me a long glance and I know that the reason has to do with me. "Anyway, he was always down for anything, even the wacky adventures and ghost hunts that you and Evan always wanted to go on. That's why we put up with Margaret."

"Put up with?"

"Well... it's wrong to speak ill of the dead."

"Cadence."

"Well, none of us liked her, even Evan wasn't that fond of her and he's far more easygoing and likes everyone. You especially hated her, gave Darryl a hard time about her all the time. At least... at first." He adds. I wonder if he's referring to the argument Darryl and I had concerning her.

"Did I have a thing for Darryl?" I ask, which would explain if I was jealous of Margaret. Cadence startles me by laughing uproariously.

"Oh no, definitely not, you liked..." Cadence stops himself and glances over.

"Darryl was like another brother. Believe me, your dislike of her had nothing to do with anything like that, you thought she was vapid and didn't think they had a lot in common..." Cadence smiles after a moment as if remembering something.

"You may not have realized it, but you were a bit of a tomboy. I don't think you have any friends that were girls at all, at least not that you were really close to. And Analise definitely didn't count as one." Well, I guess that would explain a lot, not to mention it must've been hard not to be a tomboy with a bunch of brothers.

"That isn't to say you had a problem making friends with girls or anyone in general, you and Darryl were the most outgoing in the group, it's just that you didn't spend any time with them out of school."

"So, they're more like acquaintances then."

"Yeah, I guess you could say that, anyway a bit before the accident you actually started to like Margaret a little. Well, you had it out with Darryl first." He stops and stares at me for a moment, perhaps deciding how best to word what he wants to say.

"I read a little about this in my journal. He got mad at me for being rude to her and I had to apologize and spend a day with her, right?"

"Yeah, like I said before, Darryl was a goof. I'd never seen him angry before. Heck, I'd never even heard him raise his voice. But you weren't giving her a chance. I think you thought she was going to be like Analise, you compared the two quite a bit. But after that day you were forced to hang out, well you said you found something in common with her. That was when I was a little busier with..." He trails off.

"With whatever you were hiding from me, I know, so you don't know what it was I had in common with her?" Cadence looks relieved that I don't press the issue, apparently, he's not ready to talk about whatever he's hiding and it's not like I remember enough to really confront him anyway.

"Yes, she shared your mystery obsession, you never told me, but I think you were looking into some sort of mystery with them."

We reach the front and Risa checks the books out for us, remarking on a few of Cadence's picks.

"This is, by far, my favorite book." She says as she scans one of them. It's got a black cover with a colorful and intricate one-word title, *Coalescence.*

"Mine too, I was getting it for *this* one to read." Cadence says pointing at me. I roll my eyes.

"Well, I'll read it, but don't cry when I don't like it."

"Oh no, you'll love it! It's got everything that makes a book great: action, adventure, comedy, a hint of romance, even a mystery." Risa gushes. Her love for books really is infectious.

"Ok, I'll definitely give it a shot."

"Oh, so you'll listen to her but not me?"

"Well, she's the one that works at the library. She probably knows her books, right?" I ask with a smile to let them know I'm joking.

"Of course, I'm an expert." Risa says jokingly in reply. She finishes bagging the books and tells me to let her know how I like the book before we leave.

"She's cute," Cadence says when we get to the car.

"What?" He seems surprised that he said that out loud.

"Uh... um, she's... her enthusiasm for books is cute."

"Nice try, easy now Romeo, she's at least a year or two older than you." Cadence has a blush so bright, he could stop traffic.

"Well..."

"If you say age is just a number then I'll slap you." I say.

"Can we change the subject?" Cadence asks.

I chuckle and tell him about my idea to talk with the parents of Margaret and Darryl.

"I think that's probably a bad idea, Leary, they're still in mourning."

"But they might know something." Cadence argues with me for a while but drops it when we get home.

He might be right, maybe it would be wrong to go and talk with their parents, but I can't pass it up. I decide I'll start out with Mama Etta. She already likes me at least, and I have been meaning to take up her offer for tea.

Chapter 9

"Come in dear, I'm so glad you finally stopped by. Do take off your shoes please and make yourself at home. I've a batch of scones in the oven, I'll just be a sec."

There's a whistling sound and Mama Etta bustles back toward what must be a kettle on the stove. It was surprising to find that Mama Etta lives quite close, she's practically in walking distance.

Cadence said Evan usually rode with us to school and that it wasn't uncommon to walk to the other's house to hang out. He said one time we'd somehow managed to not see Evan walking by us on the other side of the street and arrived at Mama Etta's house just to find that Evan had gone to our house.

The entire house smells like cinnamon and vanilla, and the carpet is a plushy red. I shove my sandals in with the stack of boots and sneakers by the front door that I think are probably Evan's and enter into the living room. It's exactly like what I'd imagine Mama Etta's house to be like.

There's a large fluffy looking couch and loveseat in dark shades of lilac and a sandy brown recliner with colorful pillows everywhere. There are throws draped over the back of every seat. There's a fireplace with pictures and knickknacks strewn over the mantle.

One picture in particular catches my eye. It's of a little boy, about 8 or 9, holding a puppy, that's obviously a young Evan, and what must be his parents. Little Evan still has the same brown head of curls and I'm happy to finally see the color of his eyes. Jade.

His eyes are a pale jade. All three of them are smiling happily, standing in their bathing suits, and in the background are crashing waves. It looks like Evan got his good looks from both his parents, they're beautiful, and curls definitely run in the family. If I had any doubt about who Curls was supposed to be, then it's gone now.

The woman is short, her hair a wild main of fiery curls, with a spattering of freckles and a hint of sunburn on her tanned skin. The man has the same smirk and skin as black as Mama Etta's, his hair is also a wild mass of black curls, longer than the woman's.

I'm still looking at the picture when a shaggy brown dog comes running into the room, behind the dog is Mama Etta carrying a tray laden with treats and a green kettle.

"I brought snacks." She says as she gently sits the tray down on the coffee table and takes a spot on the couch. The dog comes right to me, tail wagging like crazy and nudges my hand excitedly.

I pet the dog tentatively and he goes crazy, licking and jumping all over me.

"Sit." Mama Etta says, and he does, but whimpers at her. Over the dog's shoulder I see a flash of a grinning Evan, his arms crossed before he turns to go deeper in the house. "Sit dearie, don't mind Shakespeare. He's just really happy to see you. You haven't been around in quite a while. He's missed you."

"Shakespeare?" I ask, imagining little Evan deciding such a name escapes me. I decide to see if the recliner is as cozy as it looks and sit down, the dogs jumps in my lap and makes himself comfortable.

"My son was an English professor." Mama Etta says as she starts pouring the tea, a small smile spreading across her face. She looks towards the pictures I'd been admiring. "Evan's just lucky I talked Matthias out of naming him Hamlet. Although his middle name did end up being Lysander, couldn't talk him out of that." I can't resist the chuckle.

"Evan's middle name is Lysander?" Mama Etta nods solemnly but then starts laughing as well. It kind of fits, and it strikes me as hilarious that he auditioned for the role of Lysander when it was a part of his name. "It looks like Shakespeare remembers you, I'm sure he's missed you."

Mama Etta hands me a plate filled with treats. There's scones, a couple of cookies, what looks like a macaroon, a triangle of a cucumber sandwich, and some sort of custard looking thing along with a fruity red tea.

"So, I've met him before?" I know I have since I've read the journal entries mentioning him, but I want to know what she says.

"Oh yes dearie, you were over all the time. You and Evan have practically been inseparable since you two met. You might as well refer to yourself as Shakespeare's second human." She says with a wink. "Whenever you feel like it, it would be nice to bring Godzilla for a visit as well. The two haven't seen each other in a while."

It doesn't surprise me that the two dogs were close since we took them on hikes together, but I am a little intrigued that such a small dog would be friends with the giant that is Godzilla. Mama Etta must sense my thoughts because she pulls a picture off the mantle that I hadn't noticed.

It's of a younger version of me and Evan, both holding our dogs. Godzilla is clearly still a puppy but he's still almost half my height in the picture. He and Shakespeare are licking one another's snouts. "These two adore each other just as much as they adore the two of you."

Shakespeare nudges my hand to get me to pet him again and I'm a little impressed that he hasn't tried to get any of the food off my precariously perched plate. I scratch at his ear as I nibble on one of the scones.

"This is delicious."

"Cranberry orange, your favorite... at least it was." Mama Etta says with a sad smile.

"I think it still is." I tell her as I scarf down the rest of the scone. The rest of the sweets are just as delicious and the tea pairs well with it all.

"Go ahead and ask your questions, dearie." Mama Etta says after we've set in silence for a few minutes.

"Umm... I-I-"

"I know that's probably why you visited. I'm glad for the company, whatever the motivation may be, and I can't say that I blame you. It must be awful frightening for you, sweetie." She takes a sip of her tea as if she hasn't just practically read my mind.

"Ask whatever you need, baby."

"Umm... well... that night, the night of the accident that is... well... do... do you know anything, or well did Evan tell you what we were doing? Where we were going?" Mama Etta purses her lips and takes another sip of tea.

"I'm afraid not dear. I've always been rather lenient with Evan, never ask too many questions. And he's always been rather honest and hardworking. If I'd asked, he would've told me, but he just mentioned that he was going out with you and Darryl and his girlfriend, God rest their souls, and I didn't ask for any other details."

"What time was that?" I ask.

"Perhaps around six, I believe." Which means he left about two hours before the time the accident occurred. That still leaves the question of what we were doing near that construction site, and also what we were doing before the time of the accident.

"So, Evan didn't say anything else about what we might've been up to?" I ask. She sits forward.

"No dear, but I'm curious as to why you want to know so bad. It was just a tragic accident after all."

"Yeah, I know, but I just want to... want to understand why we were there. What were we doing near a construction site so late at night?" Mama Etta shrugs and sips her tea again.

"Now that I couldn't help you with dear. You and Evan were the curious sort though, so perhaps it was another one of your mysteries or buried treasure adventures. Or even a ghost hunt." I already knew there had to be some sort of mystery, since Cadence said we were investigating something to do with Darryl, and really, I'd been humoring the idea before he'd mentioned it, but to hear someone else point it out makes me realize that I should trust my intuition more.

Cadence did say I was obsessed with watching murder mysteries, and the fact that I hid my journal and the key to it in separate places is more than enough evidence that I had an interest in them.

"Mysteries?"

"Oh yes, you and Evan were always chasing weird stories, whether they were real or fake, or even supernatural related."

Mama Etta stares down at a bracelet on her wrist, as if lost in the memories.

"You actually had a good business one summer finding lost items together," She holds her wrist up, letting the little silver charms swing. "This was your first find. You managed to make about a two hundred a piece just helping people out. And there was the time when the two of you claimed a reward for a missing cat after hunting it down. You spent nearly a week running around with cat treats in your pockets searching for it. The strays took to following the both of you home. You both managed to rehome a few of them."

Mama Etta pauses, her eyes lighting up with a smile.

"The buried treasure is probably still the best story though."

"We found buried treasure?" She starts laughing.

"Oh goodness no, at least not real treasure at least. That brother of yours wanted to surprise you for your birthday, so he created a whole scavenger hunt for you with Evan's help. The real kicker was how the two of you actually stumbled upon a time capsule that wasn't supposed to be dug up for another ten years. You had to rebury it of course. It was quite an impressive feat for a couple of twelve-year-old's."

"Twelve? Evan and I have known each other that long?" Cadence mentioned that we'd known him and Darryl for a few years, but not how many.

"Longer dear. You two met when you were both nine, maybe ten. I believe it was the fourth or fifth grade."

No wonder I feel such a connection with him... I've been friends with him for at least six years. "You didn't like each other at first though."

"We didn't?" Mama Etta chuckles.

"I do believe you punched him in the face the first day you met him."

"What? Why?"

"For making fun of your shoes or something silly like that. I just remember that he came home with a black eye and the school suspended you for a day, but Evan retaliated and that started some sort of prank war between the two of you."

"Seriously?"

I'm trying to imagine younger me and younger Evan having a prank war in the middle of school and failing.

Mama Etta takes a long sip of her tea.

"Oh yes dear, it was quite something. See there was the time he filled your locker with confetti and you retaliated by covering his locker in sequins and glitter. Another time he glued you to a desk and then you locked him in a janitor's closet for a day. He filled your backpack with mustard while you were in gym one time, and you somehow managed to hide all of his textbooks around the school, leaving clues for him to have to hunt them down. He locked you in your locker and you zip tied his locker shut, he dropped a bucket of jello on you and you taped his backpack to the ceiling. There was more. You were both quite creative, you know."

"How were we not expelled?"

"You nearly were after you coated his desk in honey and released ants in the room."

"But we weren't?" Mama Etta lets out a guffaw.

"Your Momma talked you both out of it, I'm not sure how she did it, but it was decided that both of you would serve in school suspensions for a month, and by the end of the month the two of you were best friends."

I wonder why no one's mentioned any of this to me before.

"Would you like to see some more pictures?" She asks, already standing up and shuffling to a cabinet nearby. I move to sit next to her on the couch, which is just as fluffy as the chair and Shakespeare huffs at me before waddling off towards the kitchen. He comes back a few minutes later with a blue squeaky bone and settles at my feet.

We spend the rest of the evening with Mama Etta telling me stories about Evan, and about my friendship with him. She shows me pictures of little Evan and his parents.

I decide not to ask about what must've happened to them, not really sure how to broach the subject. And she also shows me an album worth of pictures of the two of us. Some have Darryl and Cadence in them, there's even one with everyone in the family at the beach.

There's a picture of a younger me and a younger Evan, our faces and clothes covered in dirt holding the time capsule Mama Etta mentioned. More pictures of us eating pizza and blurry pics of us in trees and climbing rocks. A pic of us at the beach, Shakespeare sitting between us, a full-grown Godzilla draped over us, and a giant sandcastle in the background. There's another one of a little Evan and I with Cadence behind us covered in snow, a half-made snowman behind us. We're all holding snowballs.

By the time I leave I haven't learned anything new about the accident, but I've learned so much more about my friendship with Evan. And it seemed like Evan was content, he sat in the chair the whole time with a wide grin on his face.

I was sort of surprised that Shakespeare didn't acknowledge him. I thought it was a thing that animals could see ghosts, but obviously not in his case and now that I think about it, Godzilla's never really noticed him either. Strange.

Chapter 10

"I can't believe I let you talk me into this." Cadence says as he rings the doorbell. We're standing in front of a two-story house straight out of a magazine.

"Well, you didn't have to come with me." I tell him. He gives me a side glance that says otherwise.

Before he can respond, a little girl opens the door. She's probably five or six, dressed in princess pajamas, with messy black hair, and red patches on her pale skin. This must be the little sister mentioned in the paper.

"MOOOOMMMMYYYY!!!!" She yells before dashing away.

"Why would she open the door if she wasn't going to say anything to us?" I ask Cadence. He just shrugs at me.

"Brooklyn, I've told you not to open the door to strangers." A woman's voice says from somewhere in the house.

An older version of the little girl comes to the door, the little girl peering at us from behind her legs. Before we can even say a word, she breaks into sobs just looking at us.

"Ummm... are you, all right?" I ask.

A scrawny man in a business suit appears behind them.

"Honey, who's at the– What are you doing here?" He asks staring at Cadence and me. He wraps the woman in his arms and the little girl clings to their legs.

"Maybe it's a bad time..." I offer.

"No, why are you here? Haven't you done enough?" The man says, he doesn't raise his voice, but it has a chilling intensity to it that's nearly worse than yelling. The woman is still sobbing uncontrollably, and the little girl starts crying too. The woman hugs the child to her to try to console her.

"Just leave, we have nothing to say to you."

"I-I just wanted to—"

"LEAVE! It's your fault our little girl is gone! All your fault!" The man yells, and the woman sobs louder.

"My Margaret, my poor little Margaret."

"I'm sorry for your loss. I just..."

"It's not her fault! You can't blame her for this." Cadence yells back. "She didn't make Margaret do anything!"

"Please, just-just leave." The man says, waving for us to go. "You've done enough." The woman buries her face in his shoulder as she cries.

Cadence looks ready to argue more, and I grab his hand to pull him away. I don't want to disturb them any more than we already have.

"Let's just go, Cadence. Let's just go." His face is just as red as it was when he faced off Analise.

"I'm really sorry we bothered you." I tell the family as I pull Cadence away.

"What the heck Cadence?"

"Margaret wasn't a little angel, she didn't even get along with her parents. She hated them."

"But still Cadence, why'd you yell at them? They're in mourning."

"They just want someone to blame, and since Evan's still unconscious and Darryl is dead, it's you."

"But that doesn't mean you need to get angry at them."

"They're acting like they're the only ones affected. They didn't even go to Darryl's funeral, nor did they bother to check on you or Evan, Mama Etta sent flowers and paid her respects to both Darryl and Margaret. Mom and Dad attended both funerals and we all spoke at Darryl's funeral. Auntie K, that's Darryl's mom, even went to Margaret's funeral and has visited Evan. Heck, we've all been visiting Evan as much as we can, even you, when you don't even remember him," Cadence's eyes are glistening, as if he might cry at any moment. "And how do they act, like they're the only ones that lost someone."

"But still that's not reason to—"

"Just drop it Lyric. I was defending you, you know." Cadence doesn't say another word as he gets in the car.

I purse my lips. "Cadence, look, I'm sorry. I shouldn't have talked you into this, I just wanted to---"

I'm not even sure what I wanted or what I expected. Even if they'd greeted me like Mama Etta, how was I to broach such a tender subject? How would I have asked them if they knew anything about the accident.

Cadence might not be entirely wrong getting mad at them for wanting to blame us for the accident, but they weren't necessarily wrong to get upset that we showed up on their doorstep.

Maybe this was a bad idea.

I just wanted to know what happened. I just want to help Evan find peace, maybe unlock my memories. It's weird that no one knows why we were there that night.

"Cadence... I'm sorry, I just..."

"No. None of this is your fault! I just can't stand how they act so self-righteous, like they're the only ones that lost something."

"Cadence, I'm still here."

"But you aren't the same! You aren't you anymore." Ouch, I knew everyone was probably thinking it, but still I didn't expect him to just say it outright.

"Seriously, you don't think that I don't know that?! It's not like I can control this! I want my memories back more than anything."

"Do you know what it was like?" He asks, clenching his fists around the steering wheel. "You were unconscious for a day, we didn't... we didn't know if you'd even wake up, and then you did, and you didn't... you didn't..." Cadence chokes back a sob.

I remember waking up. The feeling of disorientation. Being introduced to Reid, and Serenity, and the boys. Maybe it was selfish of me, but I hadn't really thought about how it must've felt for them.

"You... you didn't know us. You didn't recognize us you just... you greeted us like strangers." Cadence continues, and I feel a pang in my heart.

I'd been trying to regain my memories for me... for Evan... but maybe I owe it to them to try to remember. They'd tried so hard to help me those first few months, and I've only been focusing on my guilt that nothing has worked.

"This was a bad idea, we should've never come here." Cadence says, his knuckles turning white on the steering wheel.

Maybe it was a mistake, but we can't stop now.

"No, we're trying to get my memories back, that's the whole reason we're here. And maybe it's not working but it could."

"We should just stop... *you* should stop. This investigation, it's getting you nowhere. And it... won't." He sounds defeated.

"We've barely investigated anything! We still don't even know what happened, why we were out there, what we were looking for."

"It doesn't even matter anymore Lyric! You aren't the same, Evan's in a coma and might never wake up... and Margaret and Darryl are dead. Gone." Cadence's voice cracks on the last word.

"It doesn't matter why you were there—It won't... it won't change what happened."

He's making me mad. Doesn't he realize that I know all this? It won't bring those that died back, and it might not wake up Evan, or make me remember anything, but still I want to know, for my own sake. Regardless of the reasons, going out that night nearly killed us all. What was so important that we risked our lives for it?

"Don't you dare put that on me! Don't you think I already know that! I know I'm not the same, but that's why we should figure out what happened."

"Lyric, this isn't going to fix anything. Finding out what happened won't return you to normal!"

Normal. That word makes me clench my fists. I'm not even sure exactly what I say back, because I can barely hear him over the blood rushing through my ears. Suddenly we're both yelling at each other. I'm not even sure *what* we're arguing at this point. But I'm tired of it already. I don't like fighting with him.

"STOP IT ALREADY BEATS!" I yell. There's quiet. My heartbeat thundering in my chest, the squeal of tires as Cadence suddenly pulls the car to the side of the road. He turns to stare at me, his eyes wide.

"Y-you called me Beats. Do you-do you remember?" His gaze is so hopeful that I feel like my heart is splitting into pieces. All my anger immediately falls away.

"No... I'm sorry, I don't know why, it just kind of happened."

"Beats... you... that was your nickname for me," Cadence is crying, really crying this time, big fat ugly tears, his cheeks all blotchy. "You-you called me Beats all the time, b-but especially when you were wanting something or in the middle of an argument. Like it was your way of letting me know that you weren't really mad... even when you were. You-you really don't remember?"

I reach into the glove compartment to grab a napkin to hand to him. His nose is dripping. He takes it and blows his nose loudly.

"I'm sorry Cadence. I don't remember, I wish I did." I feel tears pricking my own eyes. I reach over the console to give him an awkward one-armed hug.

"It's fine Leary, I-I shouldn't have snapped like that, at you... or Margaret's parents for that matter. I just... they're gone, and Evan... and you... I..."

"I'd say we should go back for you to apologize but I think that would upset them more." I say jokingly, but Cadence doesn't crack a smile.

"I really shouldn't have snapped at you. I meant what I said though. It wasn't your fault what happened."

"Then who's fault was it Cadence? It wasn't their fault either."

"I'm not saying it was... it just... it was a freak accident, that's it."

"Cadence... why do you sound so guilty..."

"I don't know anything, that's what pisses me off. You wouldn't tell me where or why you were going. You said I had to either come or I'd miss out, and I couldn't get you to tell me anything... couldn't get *any* of you to tell me anything. I was supposed to be there that night. I was supposed to go, and I didn't. If I'd gone then maybe—"

"Then maybe you would be dead or comatose too." We'd broached on the subject at the scene of the accident, but it seems like Cadence is still holding on to that guilt. "Stop being like that, okay." Cadence slams a hand on the steering wheel.

"But I should've been there... or I should've talked you out of it."

"From my understanding, I'm pretty darn stubborn." I say, trying to lighten the mood.

I let out a long sigh. If just this little bit of investigating ends in an argument with the person I'm the closest to, I'm not sure I want to continue, but I think I need to.

"We should probably stop this, shouldn't we?" I ask him.

"No, maybe it would be for the best to find out what really happened that night. To figure out what all of you were hiding."

"Weren't you the one that was trying to talk me out of investigating in the first place, and just a few minutes ago too?"

"Well, yes, but now I'm not. Even if you don't remember exactly... you called me Beats. That has to mean that maybe you'll remember eventually... and maybe you're right. I wasn't really that sure before... but this investigation of yours might be the key you need to unlock your memories, and I'll help this time. I promise—" Cadence turns to look me full in the eyes, his are red rimmed and swollen. "No more bailing."

Chapter 11

"Why are we at the library again?" I ask Cadence for about the fiftieth time.

"We're going to decide our new course of action." He says plopping down into the rickety wooden seat and taking a long sip of tea.

He keeps saying that, but so far, we've just been sitting here for ten minutes with Cadence peering expectantly around us. I'm fairly certain he just wants to see Risa. And it's not like we don't have computers at home, so he can't say it's just to research the accident.

"There's not supposed to be beverages in here." I remind him.

"It's in a closed container. It's fine." I'm about to argue when a frizzy head pokes out from between two shelves and then Risa starts to walk past with a handful of books. Cadence jumps up to help, only succeeding in knocking all the books on the floor. His face is bright red as he mumbles apologies. Now *this* is painful to watch.

"Hey Risa, we're trying to plan out our next step in the mystery that is my life, want to join?" Risa checks the watch on her wrist and bobs her head.

"Sure, I can spare a few minutes. So how did meeting the parents go?" She asks. Cadence is still fumbling with her discarded stack of books and mumbling apologies, and it seems to take a moment for his brain to catch up with his mouth.

Risa already has the books gathered up and calmly reaches to take the last one that Cadence is clutching for dear life. It seems to dawn on him that Risa is trying to pull it from his hand and he awkwardly releases the book to shuffle back to our table.

"So, what about Darryl's parents?" Risa asks after I bring her up to date.

"That's a great idea. Brilliant idea! We should've thought of that. Leary, we should've thought of that. You're smart people." Cadence says. I shoot him a glance. He is acting really weird.

"I'm not so sure about it, since things with Margaret's parents went so south." I say.

"No, Auntie K is part of the family. We probably should pay her a visit. I haven't been by to see her since a little after the funeral when mom sent over a few casseroles." An expression of sadness passes briefly over his face, but at least he's finally sounding normal.

"Maybe..."

"I'll do all the talking," Cadence reassures me. He turns to give Risa a creepy smile that I think is supposed to be flirty. We are definitely going to have to discuss his flirting habits if he doesn't want to be labeled as a stalker. "Thanks for the idea again." To her credit, she doesn't seem that concerned by it.

"So... uh... how did you like that book?" Risa asks me. I'd only read the first chapter but what I'd read wasn't too terrible. The main character seemed pretty likeable and the fantasy world was described well.

Cadence chimes in about his favorite parts and then they start to ask each other about different books. I tune out as they start enthusiastically talking about their favorite authors. At least Cadence is sounding less creepy now.

I get up to walk around the books and neither even notice. When I see Evan walking past, I follow him to the screenplay section, he sits on the floor and starts to read a copy of a play, but I can't see the title. This is the first time I've seen him actually holding something, I almost reach forward to see if the book is real, like I wanted to do the last time I saw him reading. Before I can, I hear Cadence and Risa calling me. I turn towards their voices and by the time I turn back, Evan is gone.

* * *

Darryl's house looks pristine. It's a brilliant baby blue with white shutters and a large porch. Evan is swinging on the wooden porch swing out front when we arrive. An immaculate lady in scrubs answers the door at our knock. She looks to be in her early thirties and everything about her screams perfection. It makes me think of how put together Analise was. But there's something more inviting to her. Where Analise was like a cold stone statue. Mrs. Davies is like a warm summer day.

There are dark circles under her eyes and a stain on her rumpled top, indicating that the perfection is a façade. She's worn out but puts up a good front, most likely. Before we can say anything, she pushes open the door and pulls both of us into a hug. Definitely not the reaction I was expecting.

"Hi, Auntie K." Cadence says. "Mom sent another casserole." He holds out the dish to her as she ushers us inside. Serenity was ecstatic to hear that we were going to check on Karina, Mrs. Davies' first name. She insisted on sending us with food. It took a lot of convincing to only end up with one casserole and not five. "And she said not to be a stranger and to remember to call if you need anything at all."

"Oh, Serenity is such a peach, I still need to send back the dishes from the last ones she sent. Would you like some sweet tea? Water? Lemonade? I don't have soda, but I have plenty of different juices. You know the game, name a juice and I probably have it." I make a mental note to ask Cadence about that later.

"I bet you don't have banana juice." I say jokingly.

She motions us to a leather green couch that looks like it's never had anyone sit on it. Next to it are two well-worn recliners and a rocking chair.

"There's banana-apple and banana-pineapple." She says. Cadence is smirking at me.

There's an almost empty bookshelf with tons of pictures along the shelves instead of books. There's quite a few of Darryl, Evan, Cadence, and myself as children. There's one of the younger versions of the four of us, probably around 10, in bathing suits, the ocean crashing behind us.

The oldest picture of us includes Margaret, we're all covered in paint and grinning wildly. There's a family picture of Darryl and his parents. Mrs. Davies and the man are gazing adoringly at each other over top of Darryl's head.

Mrs. Davies takes the casserole into the kitchen and Cadence yells out cranberry-grape and she brings out two glasses of juice. Mine is a tan color and it tastes exactly like bananas and apples. So, banana juice is a thing apparently.

She perches on the edge of one of the recliners and reaches to take my hands. "It's good to see you walking again, dear. I've been meaning to give you a call and see how you've been doing. And you," She reaches for Cadence, "you look well. I hope you're taking good care of your sister." He nods enthusiastically.

"I've been meaning to give you this too." Mrs. Davies goes to the bookshelf and pulls out an envelope. "Just a little thank you for speaking about my baby." She's got tears glistening in her eyes. "It was a nice service wasn't it. He would've been proud."

"He would've loved the attention. We all miss him." Cadence has tears glistening in his eyes too.

"My baby always said that laughter was good for the soul and that that's why his goal was to make everyone he met laugh at least once." Mrs. Davies says.

They both begin sharing stories about Darryl. He really does sound like a fun guy and again it bothers me that I can't remember him.

Mrs. Davies turns to me.

"You really do look well, dear. Both of you do. Now I'm sure the two of you aren't just here to reminisce."

She's a sharp one. She eyes both of us with the same expression I've seen Serenity give Clef and Alto when they're goofing off too much at the dinner table.

"We had some questions." I say before Cadence has a chance to.

"About that night?" I swear this woman must be a mind reader like Mama Etta.

"Yeah, did Darryl mention where we were going or anything about what we were doing?" I ask.

She lets out a long sigh.

"I'd heard that you had some memory loss, but I just couldn't quite believe it. Oh sweetie, this must be so hard on you." She reaches to take my hand again. I think she might be the first person that I've met that responded like that.

I'm used to the looks of pity, the oohs and ahhs, and the ones that casually changed the conversation. And of course, the few people that thought I was joking at first. But she's giving me a knowing look as if she understands my pain, while nothing compared to hers, it's almost a relief to find someone to empathize with.

"I wish I could help. I really do. I was working the late shift that night and wasn't home till early morning. By that time..."

She trails off and I can practically see the scene playing out in front of my eyes. A tired and bedraggled Mrs. Davies coming home to an empty house, perhaps a phone call or a cop car showing up to inform her of the accident. She shakes her head as if to shake away the memories and purses her lips in a thoughtful way.

"Now that I think about it, all he'd mentioned was that he was going to work on a project that night, but he said he'd be back before his curfew and not to worry." She pulls a tissue out of her pocket and dabs at her eyes. "I wish that I knew more."

"No, no that's all right, we're sorry to bring it up so soon after what happened." Cadence chimes in. "We really are."

"You're all good kids, I know it wasn't anyone's fault what happened. You be good to your parents all right? They love you."

She's tearing up again. Cadence reaches over to hug her.

She gives us a lecture about staying out of trouble, I can sense what she really wants to say, though. No parent should have to bury a child. While she desperately misses her son, she's not angry that I'm still here. She doesn't blame me, and for some reason crushing guilt washes over me at the thought. I feel like she *should* blame me. Maybe not because I survived, but whatever happened that night, I'm fairly certain it was because of an idea of mine.

The conversation changes. Mrs. Davies seems like she needs to talk. I ask her about how we all met, and she tells me a hilarious story about us all meeting in a theater production during elementary school.

Apparently, there was a mix up and Darryl was given my costume, but instead of trying to figure out why someone handed him a girl's dress, he went on stage and acted my part out perfectly which left me to do his role.

The switch was done so well that everyone thought we'd planned it. After that we all became inseparable. And it helped that he lived nearby like Evan, and that he and Cadence were already friends because they played in little league baseball together.

She continues for hours telling us all sorts of stories and it's in the middle of a story about the four of us trying to build a teepee hut in the backyard with sticks, leaves, and mud that it happens. My head pounds and then I'm not just hearing her talk anymore, I *see* it. It all plays out in front of me like a movie.

It's a sunny day, and the four of us are working hard. A younger, long haired Evan has his curls tied back in a ponytail. He's making mud, using water from the hose and carefully mixing it into a bowl of dirt.

Cadence and I are dressed identically in overalls and t-shirts, something that Darryl keeps making fun of. I'm climbing up and down the large tree in the yard to pick out the perfect branches for our teepee. I've got a little gold pocket knife that I'm using to slash the branches off before taking my bundles to Darryl.

He has a bright red cast on his arm, but it's not stopping him from helping. He also has his own pocket knife, that he's using to peel the bark off the branches. Then Cadence is forming the teepee, he seems to be having trouble getting the branches to bend how he wants. Mrs. Davies interrupts to bring us bowls of ice cream and we each abandon our projects to sit on the porch swing and eat our already melting treats.

"He had a broken arm." I interrupt her story with wide eyes. This is the first thing I've truly remembered, and I savor every little detail from the hot sun, the bug bites, the rough bark, mud, and the sticky ice cream. Cadence's mouth drops open, but Mrs. Davies doesn't seem to catch the exchange.

"Oh yes. He got that from climbing the tree in the front yard." She says and then it dawns on her too, and both of them are staring at me with open mouths.

It takes everything in me not to jump up and dance from the excitement. And then I do it anyway, Cadence joins and even Mrs. Davies jumps up.

I remembered something!

Chapter 12

"Well, that's something," Alto says, folding back a page of his newspaper. It's Sunday morning, and Serenity always insists on a huge family breakfast on Sundays. Reid peers over his shoulder and lets out an agreeable noise.

"Well, that is interesting. I didn't think he had any family. Thought for sure everything would be split between the other partners." Reid comments.

"Well there was all that talk of a secret child."

"Nothing came of it though."

I tune them out for the most part, this is practically a morning ritual for them. Alto finds something noteworthy in the paper and then he and Reid discuss it.

Yesterday they were talking about a house fire in a nearby neighborhood.

Serenity places a platter of homemade biscuits and a bowl of gravy in the middle of the table. The scent of coffee wafts through the air as Clef enters with the pot and begins pouring mugs for himself, his twin, and Reid before being called back by Serenity. Cadence is right behind him and he passes me a mug of tea, still steeping.

"Assam black for this morning." He says as he sets down a little pot of cream and bowl of sugar cubes.

Harp comes rushing in then, his hair wet and mussed from his morning shower. Harp wakes up around five every morning for his run, and Serenity insists that he not come to the table sweaty. He always come running in, as if he's afraid the food will be gone. Seeing how the guys all eat, I can imagine that the food probably has disappeared on Harp before. And that's probably why Alto runs in the evenings.

"Get me a mug of that too." He says, passing Cadence. Cadence huffs but grins, he loves making tea.

Clef reenters holding a skillet of eggs and a plate of sausage links and bacon. He plops down next to Alto who's still discussing whatever piqued his interest in the newspaper. At some point he's handed off the paper to Reid.

"It says here that they're still waiting on a blood test for confirmation." Reid says.

"What are you reading?" Clef asks, glancing over.

"The late Desmond Cole, that big business tycoon, an heir has come forward." Alto says.

"Seriously? I thought the guy never married."

"He didn't, but it's supposedly a nephew from his younger sister. They were about 15 years apart and she was raised by their mother while Cole was raised by their father. Seems to be his only family."

"Hey, there's even a picture," Reid says as he turns the page.

"Wait... isn't that?" Alto glances over at Clef and looks back at the picture. He exchanges a look with Reid and bites his lip.
Sensing their looks, Clef glances over. Alto tries to hide the paper, but it's too late, he's already seen whatever it is.

Clef stands up abruptly and heads back into the kitchen, we all hear the back-door slam shut.

"What's going on?" I ask eying Cadence as he comes back in with tea for Harp along with a bowl of grilled onions, peppers, and mushrooms.

I stand up to get a look at the picture in the paper. It's a medium sized photo depicting a nondescript man with glasses and longish hair. I feel a twinge of familiarity, as if I should know who this person is and the appearance of Evan staring at the picture beside me, makes me decide to research the person later.

Alto purses his lips and stands to follow Clef.

"Let him cool off," Reid says, placing a hand on his shoulder. "He'll be back, he wouldn't miss Mom's Sunday breakfast."

As if drawn by being mentioned, Serenity comes in then, carrying a tray with a plate of fried ham, bowls of grits, a platter of fried chicken, and even a carafe of orange juice and lemonade. Fresh squeezed. They always are.

"What happened with Clef?" She asks, Reid shows her the paper. She lets out a little 'oh' and looks forlornly at the door.

"What's the deal?" I ask, hoping someone will answer me this time.

"I mentioned the she-witch with a capital B that broke Clef's heart?" Cadence finally turns to me.

"You shouldn't have mentioned her at all." Alto admonishes but Serenity shoots him a silencing glance.

"That's the guy that she was cheating with. He was working as a janitor at the hospital." Cadence says.

Clef returns at that moment and the paper is tossed away. Everything is quiet for a bit as the boys begin digging into the breakfast.

Alto starts cracking jokes to try to lighten the mood and Harp joins in. Soon everyone is laughing too hard to stay upset. Although Clef is a little quieter than normal.

When Reid pours a glass of lemonade, the twins exchange a strange look.

Serenity seems to catch the exchange and smirks, dabbing at her mouth with a napkin.

Reid takes a big gulp and spits the drink out all over his plate.

"Boys, pickle juice in the lemonade? Really?"

They all start laughing and Serenity hands a towel to Reid.

"Been awhile, you've been too complacent." Clef says. Good to see he's cheered up now.

I look towards Cadence who is hiding his laughter with a sip of tea.

"I told you there was an ongoing prank war." He says when I catch his eye.

* * *

"So, one of the janitors here is related to Desmond Cole, some big business guy that died a few months before our accident. Well, was a janitor, guess he probably quit now." I say to Evan.

I'd tried looking up the guy from the paper, but there wasn't much information about him, for a guy that's about to inherit a multimillion dollar business along with a shopping mall, three billboards, and is the sole heir of what apparently is a local icon, he's very private.

All I managed to get was the basics. Full name, Wayne Charles Wright, in his late 20's. He has a degree in chemical engineering, which makes it strange that he was working as a janitor here. Raised by a single mother, with a father spending life in prison for drug dealing, homicide, and a few other petty crimes. Up until a few months ago, no one even knew he existed.

From what I could gather, he and his mother hadn't been in contact with Cole for years. With a 15-year age difference, they weren't even close, and she was cut off from the family when she married Timothy Wright.

"And that same janitor had an affair with Analise while she was dating Clef." I look back at Evan, running my hands through his curls. "I don't know how it all connects, but there has to be something to it right? You showed up again when I saw the picture of Wright, I feel like I should know him for some reason, maybe because of the cheating thing?" I sigh.

I'd thought explaining all my worries to Evan would help but saying everything aloud just makes it even more clear that I have no idea why any of it is significant. I can't shake the feeling that it's important. I lean back in my chair and begin recounting the rest of the past few days.

"The summer will be over in about a couple of months and I've only had one memory, and you're still not awake. I really wish you'd wake up. Or at least talk to me. The séance didn't work, but I tried. I don't understand why you didn't say anything." I sigh again and lay my head on the edge of the bed, listening to the familiar sounds of the whirring machines.

"Should we just leave? Maybe this is a bad idea?" It's that voice I heard before. The one I think might be Darryl.

"Okay, okay, you're right. We should just leave then." My voice.

"Are you sure, we can... I don't know, ask someone?" Another girl's voice this time.

"And say what exactly?" Another guy's voice.

I glance over at Evan, almost afraid to even say bye, lest the voices disappear like last time. I get up quietly and make my way to the door. The voices are arguing now about how to go about looking for something. A specific room. But there aren't enough details to figure out why they're looking for a room here.

"It said that she went missing right after her shift." My voice says, okay, so that's something to look into. I make a mental note as I follow the voices.

"But a lot of what happened is just speculation."

"Well, it's not like she just disappeared into thin air, the last place she was seen was a room here." Me again.

"Have you asked Clef if he knows anything?" The other girl. I'm starting to think that this is probably Margaret, making the other male voice, Evan's.

"I would but then he'd probably get suspicious."

"And he'd say we should leave this to the police." Evan?

"But we're onto something, I know it. And what if she's still alive? She was only declared missing four days ago."

"She has a point man, maybe we can save her."

I'm really hoping for a name or something, but the voices go quiet for a second, and then when they start up again they start talking about theories on what happened.

One of the guy voices suggests alien abductions jokingly, and I'm pretty certain that one is Darryl now. He would be the one trying to lighten the mood. At some point Evan appears in front of me, sneaking along the wall

140

and I follow him. As I round a corner I smack into someone.

"Oh, Lyric darling, I have *so* been hoping to run into you." My stomach clenches as I stare at the snide grin of Analise.

Chapter 13

I stir extra cream and sugar into my hazelnut coffee while Analise is still waiting for her skim milk macchiato with extra foam and one pump of caramel. The barista's eyes practically popped out of his head when she ordered.

Evan's ghost is sitting at one of the tables and I join him while I wait for her. I'm not sure why I agreed to talk with her, but a part of me is curious as to what she wants to say.

"So, I will be frank. I know that you despised me." Analise says. She perches elegantly on the edge of her seat, her posture perfect. "And memory or not, it is clear that you know that."

"Then why were you so adamant that we spend time together again?"

"I was thinking... well hoping," she suddenly looks uncertain, the haughty expression dropping off her face makes her look younger and even prettier. "Now that your memories are gone, maybe we could start over. I think the only reason you didn't like me before was that you never really gave me a chance. The slate is empty now, perhaps you would be willing to start over?"

"But why? I didn't like you, I'm sure I had my reasons."

"I know, I know, but even though we spent time together you weren't really interested in getting to know me, you just wanted to spy on me."

"And from my understanding, I had a good reason for that. You were cheating. I suspected it and was right."

I take a sip of my coffee as I watch her expression. Her face twists a bit. I lean forward.

"So, tell me about the janitor, and tell me how you can sit there and insist you want to become friends when I'm sure you just want another *in* with Clef?" She scowls.

"Charlie... was... he was a mistake."

"That you made multiple times?"

"I don't have to explain myself to you, but... I will. Clef, he was so busy. Always so focused on his work, and Charlie was there. He wooed me and I, I let him. I was wrong about Charlie; his ambitions are more important than I am. I know it was wrong. I messed up. I really messed up, but I love Clef. I do." She sounds like she's trying to convince herself more than me. And even if I didn't already know the truth of the matter, I would still be questioning her claims.

"And I want him to give me another chance. I won't lie and say that I'm not hoping to befriend you to get close to him, but I really do care for him. I want to make amends and he won't talk to me anymore." Her voice sounds sincere, but her face says desperate.

"I saw the janitor in the paper, did you know that he was related to Desmond Cole?"

Analise shakes her head, "It was a fling, nothing more than that." Her eyes shift slightly from my face to her coffee, and I'm fairly certain she's lying, but I decide to change the subject. Maybe she'll be more forthcoming on other things.

"Tell me, what do you know about the days leading to my accident?"

Analise arches a brow and for a brief moment, so quick I'm not sure that I didn't imagine it, sheer panic crosses her features.

"What do you want to know precisely? It's not like you shared much with me." She waves her hand absentmindedly. "Getting you to talk about any of your interests was like pulling teeth. You were always questioning me and changing the subject, diverting things when I asked you any questions. All I know is that you and your little posse had some sort of mystery you were following." She waves her hand again, "You were certain that you knew what happened to this missing nurse from the hospital."

"Right, the nurse, what was her name again?" So, that's the *her* the voices were referring to

"Jeanette Waters, and *no* I did not know her personally. Neither did you for that matter, but you made some sort of connection. Now are you willing to start over or..."

My face must answer her question because she leans forward and drops the sincerity again, this time it's all desperation.

"Please, please give me another chance, help me get back with him."

"Why are you so obsessed? You weren't even with him for that long, and you cheated on him, sorry that I don't quite believe in your supposed devotion. My loyalty is to my brother, after all. And according to him you were having a fling with *Charlie* before you ever asked him out." Her eyes grow wide, an alarmed look taking over.

"I'm pregnant." It clicks then, the distress in her face.

Analise seems the type that craves perfection, from her pristine appearance to her ramrod straight posture. Being a single mother probably doesn't fit her image. It raises another question, is Clef even the father?

"So, the father is?" Her eyes shift again. Whatever she says next, I bet will be a lie, so I keep her from saying anything. "You don't know do you?"

"There's a chance—"

"Don't even start with that wishy-washy attitude, tell me honestly. How *certain* are you that the father could be Clef? Is there any chance?" I cut her off before she can respond again. "Any chance at all? Would you be willing to have a paternity test to prove that it's his kid?" She won't look me in the eye now.

145

I can't understand how this girl thought she could get away with cheating, she's so obvious about it. But then again maybe it's another ruse to gain sympathy. Poor pregnant Analise, about to be a single mother. If there was even a chance it was Clef's kid, then I'm sure she would've told him already. He doesn't strike me as the type to abandon a child.

"Does the janitor know? Did you tell him? It's his kid, right?"

She bursts into tears then, and call me heartless, but it solidifies my anger even more. She brought all this onto herself and a few tears won't sway me.

"He called me a whore. He said he wanted someone better than me, someone that has more *substance*. As I said... he has ambitions, and I don't fit into them."

"He's got a point. You haven't answered my question. Is the kid the janitor's?"

She chugs her coffee, tears still falling.

"It's his, it's his kid, and he doesn't want anything to do with it. That bastard said I might as well get rid of it." She's an ugly crier, her face turning red and blotchy. Snot dribbles down to her chin.

"So that's why you started harassing Clef, you got the bright idea that you'd pass the kid off as his?" She just continues to cry.

"You sit there and have the audacity to claim you love Clef. You don't love him, you just want him to help you keep your image. You love the idea of him. I admire that you seem to want to keep the baby at least but," I stand up to leave. "Do yourself and the kid a favor and put it up for adoption."

"Lyric, I'm sorry, I really am. I –"

"Don't start. I don't believe anything you say. I don't think I ever did." Just as I reach the door I turn to glance at her. "And stay away from my brother."

Chapter 14

"So, what exactly are you wanting to find this time?" Cadence asks, he swivels around in his chair next to me. He keeps eying the shelves around us, obviously on the lookout for Risa again.

"Jeanette Waters, anything we can find out about her." I also want to try looking up the janitor a little more, but I don't want to let Cadence know about that just yet. I decided on the library computers because I don't want to leave a trail to our house until I know more of what's going on. Maybe I'm being paranoid but there's something weird about all of this.

There's a nagging feeling in the back of my mind about that janitor too, but I'm not sure why or how it would connect to everything else if it even does.

"Did I miss something? Who's Jeanette Waters?" I have Cadence's full attention now. I point to the computer in front of him.

"Google her and get back to me. I think I was investigating her disappearance."

"Did you... did you remember something?" Cadence keeps his voice even, but that glimmer of hope is still there.

"Not quite, I actually ran into Analise and finagled some information from her."

"That witch? What did she want?"

"I'll tell you later, the library closes at nine, so research."

Cadence lets out a huff, but I hear typing a few seconds later.

I start out with searching the janitor again. Once more, I hit a dead end as far as anything new. The guy's practically a ghost, not even a social media presence. Other than the small article about his possibly inheriting Desmond Cole's sizable estate, there's no other information about him.

According to the article there's no guarantee that he'll even inherit anything because Cole's will disappeared. The last it was seen, everything was going to his partners and any remaining family. So, as his only living relative he stands to gain most of the estate.

But as Reid mentioned the other day, there's a bunch of speculation about a secret child. The business partners said they are willing to wait for Cole's "secret heir" to appear before the estate is split up, and there's quite a bit of legal battling due to the fact that Wright doesn't want to wait.

I only find one article that talks about the secret heir that Reid and Alto mentioned. Cole told his business partners to be prepared to meet someone when he got out of the hospital. And his lawyer supposedly claimed Cole had recently changed his will and sent it to this secret person.

The whole story sounds a little farfetched, though. The writer doesn't have any legit sources and only a few reaching quotes from Cole's lawyer and one of his business partners.

Out of slight curiosity I start researching Desmond Cole instead. I'd already read a little about everything the guy owned, but the guy was seriously loaded. Besides being a wealthy business owner, he was well loved in the community for funding several charities. He had a soft spot for orphans and had been known to foster children when he was younger. He donated to the art programs at all the local schools and was a major contributor to fixing up one of the parks.

The park in question, called The Hill Creek Gardens, is planning on putting up a plaque in one of their gazebos to honor Cole. His funeral was massive, with people flying in from all over the country to pay their respects and even the city's Mayor made an appearance.

I stumble upon an article right about a month before he was hospitalized that announces his plans to build a new mall. Dated a few weeks before he died of a stroke is another article announcing the postponement of all building plans, pending Cole's recovery. He was in the hospital for some procedure, but the article doesn't state what. A picture at the side of the article shows the no trespassing signs outside of a building site.

"Hey Cadence, this is where my accident was, isn't it?" I ask him.

He glances over briefly.

"Yeah, it looks like it," he scrolls through the article.

"So, the question is, why were you at the closed construction site for the new mall?"

Yeah, just another weird mystery to solve. As if to add to the situation, I glimpse Evan over the top of the computer smiling in my direction.

Cadence sits back into his seat and motions me to look at the article he's reading.

"So, Jeanette Waters, 25-year-old nurse at Silver Pines General Hospital. She was reported missing by her sister after she didn't come home one Thursday night. She was last seen leaving her shift at the hospital around 5:00pm. She had a night class to go to at 6:00 but she never showed up to it. She still hasn't been found, and there's a hotline to call if anyone has information about her disappearance."

Accompanying the article is a picture of a curly headed woman wearing wide rimmed glasses.

I scan the story. "So, she's been missing for almost four months and the police couldn't find any leads."

"You think that the accident had something to do with her disappearance?"

"I don't know, maybe. Analise isn't the most reliable source but she said that we were investigating it."

"So maybe we should reinvestigate it? We can start with talking to the sister."

"Wouldn't that be a little crass? Her sister is missing, I doubt she'll want to talk to a couple of kids."

But it's the only lead we have.

* * *

A little girl with wild curly hair, holding a raggedy stuffed dragon opens the door.

"Auntie Mo!" The girl calls. A frazzled looking woman in her early 20's comes rushing to the door. She pauses when she sees us. There are dark circles under her eyes and it looks like she hasn't washed her hair in days.

"You again?" She says with a glance in my direction. "Lyric, right?" That's probably a good sign.

"You know me? I mean... sorry if this is weird... we don't mean to bother you or anything but—" It had been rather easy to find Mora Waters address. There was another article that mentioned her name and she was in the phonebook.

She motions for us to come inside.

"Sadie why don't you show them to the den, I'll get some snacks."

She returns a few moments later with a plate of fruit and juice boxes.

"Sorry, not much but water and juice to drink. I read in the paper about your accident. I'm glad to see that you're okay."

"So, we came here before?" I ask leaning forward to pick up a juice box. The little kid sits in the floor in front of one of the couches and starts eating some of the grapes.

"Well you and a few others, not him." She points to Cadence. "But another girl, umm Margaret and two boys. You and Margaret did most of the talking though. What brings you back?" She asks.

"That accident you read about... I lost my memory in it." I decide to get right to the point. A look of understanding crosses her face.

"The only thing I can tell you is that you were investigating Jeannie's disappearance."

"What did we know? What did you tell us?"

"Honestly, I didn't ask. And I told you kids to leave things to the cops."

"So, we've got nothing." Cadence says.

She lets out a sigh and levels her gaze on me.

"I admire that you kids wanted to help find my sister. The cops just brushed over it, they tried to find her, they did, I'll give them that, but when no evidence came to light they just gave up." She runs a hand through her messy hair and reaches over to grab a juice box.

"It's still an open investigation, but they don't have the 'resources,'" here she uses air quotes, "to continue actively looking for her, but Jeannie would never of just up and run away. She was working hard at the hospital and she was studying to further her career."

Here she glances over at Sadie who's moved to the side of the room and is playing with the dragon and a few other toys. "And she never would've run off on her daughter."

The article hadn't mentioned anything about a daughter, but I can see the resemblance now that it's been mentioned.

"Was there anything that happened beforehand maybe, or an indication that she was, I don't know, seeing someone or something?"

She starts laughing suddenly, one of those almost hysterical laughs that happen when a person hasn't laughed in a while.

"You asked the same thing back then, just like the detectives. You and the other kids sounded just like mini detectives you know, but no, she wasn't seeing anyone as far as I know... but she was... she was upset about something. She said she was having drama at work but wouldn't go into any details. Any career in the medical field is stressful, especially when any of your patients die."

Cadence and I exchange glances, that's definitely something to look into.

"Wait one of her patients died? Was it Desmond Cole by any chance?"

Her brow wrinkles at the name and she shakes her head no.

"No, it was an aging widow. She only mentioned it once, she didn't say that it bothered her or anything like that, but I could tell that it was upsetting her. It was the first patient she had that died. And her work issues started soon after. She was stressed, working full time, trying to focus on her studies and take care of Sadie, she never would've up and left."

"So, the work drama, she didn't go into any details at all?"

"Like I said, she was stressed, she came home later after her classes a few times, and once I found her on the phone angrily yelling at someone, but she wouldn't tell me what was going on. She just said it was work stuff and that she would deal with it. Jeannie was private like that." She glances over at Sadie again and gives a wry smile.

"She never even told me who Sadie's father is. Just said he wasn't worth knowing. I have my suspicions, of course, but... well that just shows she kept most things to herself."

"Did you tell the police about any of that?" Cadence asks.

"Maybe it had something to do with the father?" I add in.

She lets out a harsh laugh and adamantly shakes her head.

"Of course, I did. They even pulled her phone records, but the number was from a payphone, can you believe those things still exist? And as for Sadie's father, I was under the impression that he doesn't know about her. But I really don't think it had anything to do with him, because if he's who I think, then he doesn't even live in the state anymore. The police humored the idea that she had a secret boyfriend, and maybe she did, but the phone calls I overheard... those didn't sound like a lover's quarrel."

Jeanette Waters had a secret, that much is clear, and I'm going to figure it out.

Chapter 15

When we get up to leave, Mora Waters pulls me into a tight hug. I feel a little dejected, I was really hoping to find out more information from her, but it's nice to know I'm on the right track.

"You're a good kid. Thank you for caring so much about Jeannie." She backs up to smile at me. "She would've liked you."

She says it in a way that makes it seem like she's given up. It's been months since Jeanette disappeared after all, at this point the chances that she's still alive are slim, and that sours my mood further. To get so close, to meet yet another dead end, it's aggravating. What did past me find?

"I know!" Cadence says suddenly, breaking the silence.

"Know what?"

"What we should do." He says with a grin.

"What? More research? Maybe, there has to be *something* we're missing. We were obviously on to something and it has to do with Jeanette Water's disappearance, but what connection could we have possibly made that the police didn't? And does it connect to Desmond Cole? Does it even connect to him?"

I just can't quite put my fingers on it, but my instincts are telling me that I must've found something.

"Well the easy explanation to that is what her sister said. The cops didn't take her disappearance seriously. Mora did say they thought she'd run off with a boyfriend or something."

I think of Jeanette's kid and how adamant Mora was that her sister wouldn't abandon them, as well as her denial of Jeanette having a boyfriend.

"But if Mora is right and she didn't have a boyfriend then there's something else going on."

"She could've been hiding one. Just because they're sisters doesn't mean that they shared everything. And Mora even said that Jeanette was extremely private." I think of the secrets I seem to have had from my brothers. He has a point there.

"True, but that still doesn't explain her abandoning her kid."

"All right I concede, but that actually wasn't what I was referring too. You need to take your mind off everything."

This is said with a glance over at me as Cadence pulls the car onto the freeway. He doesn't say anything else for the remainder of the ride, turning the volume up on some smooth jazz band that perfectly fits his personality. When he finally pulls into our driveway he gives me instructions to grab some closed toed shoes and a swimsuit.

"Either your hiking boots are the sneakers!" Cadence yells as he runs off.

As I'm hunting through my closet, Harp appears in my doorway, still in his pajamas and yawning wildly.

"What's up? Cadence is like a whirlwind in the kitchen right now. I tried to grab some juice and he threw an orange at me."

"Are you just now waking up?" I ask, glancing over at him as he yawns again.

"Yeahhh... was playing video games all night." He replies sheepishly. "So, what's going on?"

"No clue, Cadence just said to grab a swimsuit and either my hiking boots or sneakers. Apparently, we're going somewhere to clear our minds, his words, not mine."

Harp's face suddenly lights up and I can only assume he knows what Cadence has planned. Without another word he runs off. I look to where Evan is sitting nonchalantly at my desk, "I wonder if you know what they're thinking? Care to share?" He doesn't respond of course, but it's rather comforting to talk to him.

It doesn't take long to find a dozen or so suits folded in one of the drawers. Either I really liked to swim or had some kind of obsession with swimsuits. They're all different styles, with the exception of the yellow.

There's a one piece black and yellow striped suit that makes me think of a bumblebee, and then a couple of two-pieces, one with black shorts as the bottoms and the other with a little yellow skirt and then two black and yellow bikini tops.

"Seriously what was up with my love of yellow?" I settle on the bumblebee suit and pull on a pair of yellow shorts and a white tank top. In contrast to my wide variety of suits I own only seven pairs of shoes, a pair of black flats that I assume are my dressy shoes, hiking boots, combat boots, two sandals, flip-flops, and a pair of well-worn sneakers. I grab the sneakers.

By the time I make it to the kitchen Cadence has a cooler bag that looks like it's filled to the brim and Harp is beside him with another bag. They're both already wearing their swimsuits and grinning like they've got a secret. Godzilla seems to sense it too and tries to follow us out the door.

"Next time Zill." Cadence says to him, scratching behind his ears.

Throughout the drive neither Harp or Cadence will reveal anything but given the food and swimsuits I'm guessing we're heading to the beach, probably the same one I mentioned in my journal. Although they're both wearing hiking boots and wearing those to the beach is a bit odd, so maybe I'm wrong.

It isn't long before Cadence is pulling onto a dirt road in the middle of the woods, so apparently, I'm way off. The shoes make sense now. As soon as Cadence pulls the car into park, Harp jumps out with an excited yell and takes off into the woods.

"What's up with him?"

"Oh, he does that every time, he knows where we're going, so he'll be fine." Cadence gives me a look, one of those looks that make my heart ache a little, that speaks of so many things I can't remember.

"We... we haven't been back since," he glances at me as if trying to gage my reaction. "Since... well... you know. This, this was one of our spots." He says with a sad smile.

I thought they'd already taken me to all the places we liked to spend time, but this is new. I try to quell the hopeful excitement that springs up. Nothing else has worked, so why would this? I'd pretty much stopped all hope before that sliver of memory at Darryl's house.

There's something about the light shining through branches of trees to create little shimmering pockets through the forest. Something about the summer sun beginning to blare down, the smell of moss and dirt, the sound of birds and wind through leaves. It's more than peaceful, it feels like I'm home. For the first time since I woke up, I feel like I belong somewhere. I look to see Cadence watching me with a twinkle in his eyes

"Just wait till we get to the best part!" He leads me through the forest up a slope until we reach a creak.

"All right we're going to have to cross here, follow my lead."

There's stones scattered throughout the water. Cadence takes his time testing each one before putting his full weight on them, a few shift beneath my feet as I follow but I manage to keep my balance. After we cross, Cadence gives me another wide grin.

I follow him up another path that continues to slope up, after a bit of walking we get to a part where the dirt path narrows and to the right is a drop of a few hundred feet covered in brush and trees.

Cadence carefully picks his way up over roots and fallen branches, the weight of the cooler bag not even bothering him. We pass through a small clearing bathed in a patch of light with a few flowers here and there.

For a while the only sounds are of the distant trickling of water, the rustling of leaves, and the crunch of branches underfoot. It's peaceful, I could lay on the path right now, and I think I'd have a better sleep than I've had since I woke up in the hospital.

"So where exactly are we going?" I'm not sure why, but I'm whispering, as if this place is sacred. Another grin is my answer. Cadence waves the question away and continues down the trail.

We come out of the trees to another uphill path. When we reach the peak, I can see that some of the roots and rocks descend into natural steps. The creek we crossed earlier is peeking through the trees at the bottom of a steep drop.

There's a few more up and down slopes but they're growing less elevated the farther up we go, and the air is tinged with the smell of water. A light breeze picks up as we finally reach a portion of forest where dirt makes way to more rock. Two large trees growing at an angle overhang an expanse of water.

The creek that we crossed streams into a large pool hemmed in by trees and rocks. A giant boulder sits to one side, half buried in the water. On top of it, legs swinging, is Harp.

"Ya'll are so slow!" He shouts. I can see he's stowed his gear on some of the rocks below. He dives into the water with an excited shout and wades towards us. Cadence is already unlacing his shoes as Harp gets out and shakes the water off.

"Had to take Leary the long way, of course."

Saying this place is gorgeous feels like an understatement. The trees practically float over the glassy water, moss spread up their trunks. The slippery rocks are the color of copper and reflect the clear sky above us. A wind teases my hair as I take in the pool. I watch Cadence join Harp in the water, the two splashing one another. They race to the rock and both climb up it to jump. They seem to realize that I need a moment to take it all in.

And then on the rock, right after Cadence jumps, I see another person.

Evan.

I've never paid attention to what he was wearing before. It hadn't occurred to me that a ghost could even change clothes. But now he's in swim trunks, light shining on the water dripping down his bare chest. His curls are plastered to his face and he's holding his arms in the air with the widest smile. He's beautiful and I gasp a little at the sight.

162

The him in the hospital and in his pictures, it doesn't compare to the image I'm seeing now. As if he was carved from stone, a halo of light streaming around him. But there's something so sad about seeing him there. My chest aches with a longing I don't fully understand, and I push it to the back of my mind as I watch him.

He lowers his head and looks straight at me, raising goosebumps on my arms. He gives me a thumbs-up and cannonballs into the water. I watch where he landed, half expecting a splash. I realize after a moment I've been holding my breath, waiting to see him surface, and then I'm seeing others. Darryl and Margaret are chasing each other through the water, she pulls ahead and splashes a sleeping Cadence. That causes me to take a step back. I glance from the image of Cadence as he gets up and towels water off his head, and back to the real Cadence, who is climbing up the rock again.

It's eerie, as if he's in two places at once. Ghost Cadence turns to where I am and gives me a smirk and I see he's not looking at me but behind me. My whole body feels like someone just poured water on me and I turn to see a laughing Evan.

"Hey, you coming in or what?" The image of Evan disappears at Harp's shout. I glance down and realize I'm not dripping water.

It was my imagination. Just my imagination, I tell myself. But I can't shake the feeling that I'm wrong. I saw and felt something that wasn't happening. And it's not like that's the first time, either.

Chapter 16

Cadence calls us out of the water to eat and when he pulls out two of the sandwiches and tosses one at me Harp makes a disgusted face.

"You really made those? She probably won't even like 'em now." I eye the sandwich he passed to me. It looks like it has peanut-butter and something chocolate on it.

"This used to be our favorite outdoor snack." Cadence says. He won't meet my eyes as he says it, staring down at the sandwich in his hands instead. He unwraps it carefully, as if the sandwich itself is just as precious as whatever he's remembering.

"What kind of sandwich is it?" I ask tentatively. I've already learned that Cadence and I seemed to have had unique tastes.

Harp starts laughing.

"You were about 5 at the time." Cadence says.

"And I was hungry and crying." Harp chimes in.

"Mom and Dad were outside working in the garden together and you didn't want to bother them, so you said you'd make a snack." Cadence finally meets my eyes, his gaze tinged with sadness and humor. "You were trying to make peanut-butter and jelly, but you couldn't find the jelly, so you used something else instead and then added half a banana. You said it would make it healthy."

Harp is laughing so hard his eyes are teary now. I finally unwrap the sandwich to see what's on it.

"Chocolate?" I ask, lifting the bread up.

Cadence motions for me to take a bite. It's extremely sweet.

"Icing. It's chocolate icing." I say with my own laugh. It's not bad. I do have a sweet tooth after all. Harp makes a gagging face. I guess it would make sense that he didn't like it.

"You don't have much of a sweet tooth do you Harp?" I ask. I see his sandwich actually *is* peanut-butter and jelly.

He tosses me a bottle of water as he scarf's down his food.

"Not really, I think I'm the only one in the whole family who couldn't eat a whole cake in one sitting."

"It's because when he was little he got into the pantry and ate three full packages of cookies when everyone was sleeping." Cadence says.

"I was sick for days after," Harp says sheepishly. He ducks his head down as he starts pulling little bags of veggies and fruit from the cooler. He tosses me a bag of celery and another bag of strawberries.

"By the way I noticed you wore the bumblebee suit." Harp says. I think he's just trying to change the topic from himself, but I decide to let him.

166

"Yeah, what was up with all the black and yellow suits? I know yellow was my favorite color but seriously...."

"You actually liked the fact that it made you look like a bumblebee. It was your favorite suit. You said it was a great deterrent for perverts hitting on you at the beach."

"How so?" Sometimes I can't quite understand what I must have been thinking, but I have to admit I was extremely sassy and entertaining. So, whatever my reasoning, it was probably hilarious.

"Whenever a guy hit on you by saying something about how gorgeous you were, you would tell them—" Cadence stops to laugh, the same kind of uproarious laughter Harp was doing earlier.

"You would tell them, 'I'm a bee. BZZZZZZ,'" Harp chimes in in-between chuckles.

"And then you'd start running around with your arms flapping wildly and buzzing the whole time." Cadence wipes tears from his eyes.

I throw my bag of celery at him. "I didn't?!?"

"Oh, you most definitely would. You said if a guy could only compliment you on your looks then it didn't matter how you acted. Not all compliments, of course. Just the compliments that only had to do with physical attributes."

"Oh my gosh, how did they react?"

"Oh, well most of them would run off nearly as fast as they could. But not surprisingly you actually had a few that thought it was so hilarious that they still asked for your number."

"Well, only the ones that Cadence and Evan didn't scare off." Harp says with another laugh. Cadence throws the celery at Harp.

"Why would the two of you scare them off?" I ask.

Cadence purses his lips and shakes his head.

"Well, obviously Evan would because—"

Cadence tackles Harp before he can finish.

"We couldn't be the fifth wheels after all. We already had Darryl and Margaret making goo goo eyes at each other."

"But what about mmmph..."

"Eat some more carrots Harpy, you need to keep up your strength." Cadence says after having shoved a handful of carrots into Harp's mouth. Harp chews them and rolls his eyes at me.

When we finish eating we dive back into the water, taking turns jumping off the rock. Harp swings from some of the trees into the water and after a while Cadence stretches out and sunbathes.

I'm thankful that I don't see the ghosts again, and I have to keep reminding myself that it was just my imagination, but I'm not so sure. After all Cadence isn't dead, so I can't think of why I'm seeing his ghost. Is it his ghost? It probably was just my mind playing tricks on me.

Cadence's phone starts ringing as we start getting ready to hike down before the sun sets.

"Hey Mom, yeah they're with me, what's up?" Harp and I edge closer to him. He drops the cooler and turns to stare at us. "Y-yeah, I'll tell them. We'll be there as soon as possible." He ends the call and stares at us for a second, tears brimming in his eyes.

"What's wrong?"

"It's... it's Evan." My heart sinks.

No, no I'm not ready. He can't be....

"Is he?" Cadence is shaking his head and I can see he's smiling through the tears. He pulls me and Harp both in for a hug and suddenly lets out a couple of excited shouts.

"He's... awake... He's awake!"

And we're all crying now. The three of us shout our gratitude to the trees.

"HE'S AWAKE!"

Chapter 17

"He's asleep right now, you'll have to come back tomorrow."

Those words shouldn't fill me with relief. Evan's awake. We were so close to being able to talk with him again. To see him at least, even if we couldn't talk.

We were so excited, but the thought of talking to him at this moment, it terrifies me. I can see the opposite in the eyes of my brothers. Cadence looks like he might start crying again and Harp is already bawling. If I had any doubt as to how much they cared about Evan, well I don't now.

Apparently, Serenity and Clef were the only ones that made it in time to see him besides Mama Etta, and even Mrs. Davies showed up for a few minutes, Clef told us.

Mama Etta and Mrs. Davies have already gone home, and Clef went back to his shift. So, it's just us standing near the nursing station next to Serenity.

"You can come back tomorrow," Serenity is saying as thundering steps echo down the hall. Reid and Alto appear at the end of it.

"How is he?" Reid asks, he's got a handful of flowers and Alto is carrying a basket filled with a strange assortment of things from chocolate and peaches to toy cars and books. There's even a stuffed bumblebee in there. I'm not sure whether to start laughing or crying at the weird get-well basket.

Then again, Cadence made us stop and bought a bag of sunflower seeds and a magazine about gardening, and the basket at least has fruit, so maybe it's the more normal of the two.

Their crestfallen faces when Serenity repeats the same thing the nurse just said to us is heartbreaking. I feel another wave of guilt for feeling so relieved.

It's not that I don't want to see Evan. I do. I desperately do. The doctors had already warned us that if he did ever wake up there might be other things to worry about, and now the moment of truth is here.

I did my own research on comas too, we're lucky he even woke up. He scored so low on the Glasgow Coma Scale, and most people in that deep of a coma end up in a vegetative state. Now that he's awake, what damage did the car crash really do to him? There could be all sorts of brain damage that we won't be able to know about until after he's gone through tests.

What if he doesn't remember me? That thought nearly makes me sick, but then, what if he does? I almost think it might be worse if he does. I've felt so comfortable with him partly because I didn't have to deal with that look my family gives me, that desperate hope that every little thing might jog my memory.

I should be more excited that the one person that was there that night is awake, but what might he say? What if he hates me for what happened? And what am I going to say to him? What do you say to someone that you feel a connection to but don't remember?

I only know Evan through the stories that Mama Etta, my brothers, parents and even my journal have told me, but what will happen now that he's awake? Will that connection still be there?

"We'll see you kids at home," Serenity says suddenly. I realize I haven't been paying attention at all to her prognosis of Evan. She gives the boys hugs and stops at me.

"No matter what, it'll be all right." She says as if she can see all the worries gnawing at my mind. She pulls me into a hug and then walks off. Reid and Alto give dejected glances to us and follow her out.

"I guess we should go." Cadence says, pulling me away. I notice Harp is already gone and realize he must've left with the others.

"Wait, I think we should talk with one of the nurses."

"Mom already told us how he was." Cadence says, arching a brow.

"No, about the other thing, Jeanette."

"Oh... oooh. Okay, I'll go to the other nursing station, you ask questions here." Cadence rushes off without another word. I think the idea of a task is giving him something to focus on, I know it's helping me.

I make my way over to the nurse and realize its Bridget again. Perfect. She's chatty enough that she'll probably tell me something with little prompting.

"Hey Bridget," I say with a smile and wave.

"Oh Lyric, dear, I heard Evan woke up! Isn't that wonderful." It should sound like a question, but she says it as if there's no other way for it to be.

She gives me that heartwarming smile again and it's a balm on my senses. I almost feel bad that the only reason I'm talking to her is to find out information. She really does seem like a sweet person.

"Yes, we didn't get a chance to see him today, but hopefully sometime tomorrow."

We chat amicably for a few minutes before I try to casually mention Jeanette. I probably don't need to be so cautious, Bridget isn't the type to get suspicious.

"Oh right, you were asking about her before your accident too." Bridget says.

"I was? With Evan and two others, right?" She nods and purses her lips as if thinking.

"I'm not sure I remember what I said, but I didn't know her very well. She kept to herself. There was a rumor about her though."

"A rumor?" I ask. I try desperately to keep my excitement toned down. I don't want her to know how much I need this information.

"Just that she was seeing someone at the hospital. But she was real secretive about things. And well everyone loves to gossip here. It's almost as bad as high school. Get seen talking to someone once and the rumors fly." That's completely opposite to what her sister thought. Interesting.

But as Bridget said, it could just be a rumor. The fact that she's uncertain whether to believe the gossip amps up my opinion of her.

"Someone else I talked to mentioned her losing a patient not long before she disappeared."

Bridget gets that thinking face again.

"It's a hospital... sadly, we lose a lot of patients." She says this with such a heartbroken look, as if she's responsible for all of them.

"It was the first one she lost, from my understanding." Bridget shakes her head.

"Sorry, I can't really think of anything."

"How about Desmond Cole?" I'm probably pushing my luck with this one, but there must be something.

"Oh, that was such a tragedy wasn't it?" I nod. "You know he was set to be released only three days before his stroke. It was just so sudden, there was nothing we could do." She looks like she's going to start crying, so I change the subject to something lighter.

By the time Cadence has returned I've learned that Bridget owns three lizards, collects water samples from different parts of the world, and likes hockey.

"You find anything?" I ask.

"The only thing I could figure out was about the patient her sister mentioned."

Cadence looks slightly dejected, so whatever it is, must not have been what he was expecting.

"The patient she lost was an aging widower, no family and only a couple friends that would visit her. She was in extreme pain and already dying, it was just a matter of when."

That... sucks.

"So, it was expected?"

"Apparently."

"I wonder why it ate away at Jeanette so much then, if she knew it was going to happen eventually."

"The nurse said Jeanette was the last one there with her when she died, she saw it happening, was holding her hands as she took her final breaths. Something like that would probably mess with anybody." I nod.

"Well, according to hospital gossip, it was believed that Jeanette had a secret lover on the hospital staff."

"That is definitely different than what her sister thought."

"Well, it is just a rumor, so who knows if there's any validity. It could be that she just had a close guy friend or something."

Seeing how I didn't have any friends that were girls, with the exception of Margaret,

I'm willing to give her the benefit of the doubt.

"True but I'm betting that if we figure out who the rumored guy was, then we'll be one step closer to discovering what happened."

"But she didn't really have any friends on staff from what I gathered. How are we going to find anybody that knows who she might've been seeing?"

It seems that the more we try to unravel what was going on, the more questions that arise. Who was Jeanette supposedly seeing? And why would her sister be so certain that she wasn't seeing anyone? And how does Desmond Cole fit into everything? Or does he? Maybe that's completely unrelated, but again I get that needling feeling in my gut that the death of Desmond Cole has something to do with this too.

"For now, we should go home so that we can get up early to visit Evan in the morning." Cadence says. I kind of wish he hadn't reminded me.

Chapter 18

"Evan's in the paper." Alto says by way of greeting when I come down for breakfast. He shows me a small article in a side column of the paper. It's just a blurb really, they refer to him as a miracle survivor, and mention that he woke up. But it's the article beside it that really catches my attention.

A will for Desmond Cole was finally found, leaving all of his estate to any surviving relatives. And the partners have finally agreed to stop waiting on a secret child to appear. So, the only protentional heir has now become the official heir, interesting.

There's a small bit of information explaining that the will needed to be authenticated first but having been found in the midst of his possessions it's strongly believed the will is legit. After that the article recaps what I already know about the former janitor but with one interesting addition.

"Is that Analise?" I ask pointing to the small black and white photo showing a candid shot of Wright leaving the hospital next to a slightly blurred woman. She's not as willowy as Analise, but I want to be sure.

"It doesn't look like her, no. Hmmm, maybe he was seeing someone else too."

"Maybe," I reach for the paper, "Can I borrow this for a few minutes."

"I've already read all of this page, so you can have it." Alto hands me the article about Desmond Cole's will and I rush to my room. I can't be certain just yet, but I think I know who the woman in the photo is.

Underneath the photo it says it was submitted by an anonymous source. I wonder if Wright submitted it himself to increase his popularity. I remember finding a magnifying glass in my desk when I was searching for my journal key that could help me see the image a little better.

Using my phone, I pull up a photo of Jeanette Waters and use the magnifying glass to compare the two of them. It's close enough that it could be her. The photo is too grainy to really make out their facial expressions, but their body language doesn't say lovers. She's turned slightly away as if ready to leave as soon as possible and his stance seems agitated.

I'm not sure how it's a clue, but there's got to be something to it. This is the connection I was looking for. I'm not sure why I was so certain there was a connection but I'm a little satisfied that I've found one now.

* * *

Arriving back in the hospital with the knowledge that the person I'm here to visit is awake, it's a different feeling. It's like suddenly time has jumped forward.

Visiting Evan had always seemed so relaxing, and quiet, almost timeless, but suddenly I'm more aware of the bustling nurses, the squeaky wheels of carts, the whirring of machines and TVs. Walking down the hall, I can feel my heart accelerating.

This is the moment I've been waiting for and dreading. I'd almost be relieved if we were sent away again, but no one stops us as we reach Evan's door.

Through the cracked open door, I can see those of my family that are already here. Mama Etta, Serenity, Reid, Alto, and Clef surround the bed, my view of Evan is blocked by Alto's back. They're all teary eyed. Mama Etta is dabbing at her eyes with a tissue and talking animatedly with Serenity and Reid. The whole room is filled with balloons, stuffed animals, flowers, and baskets.

Cadence's sunflower seeds and magazines are not the weirdest things in the assortment. There's a basket filled with jars of what look like sand, and another one that has nothing but cans of liquorice. Evan must have some eclectic interests. Cadence and Harp rush around me and dive straight to the bed. Only a last-minute movement from the twins keeps them from tackling Evan.

"Easy there, you don't want to send him back under when we finally got him back, do you?" Clef says it with a slight smile, but there's an edge under it, showing how serious he is.

I'm about to step in the room, when Alto moves just enough for me to see Evan. He glances from the brothers and then looks towards me. My feet lock in place and I suddenly feel that the merest breeze could knock me over. Cadence is bawling and laughing at the same time, rambling about all sorts of things to Evan and while I can tell he's listening, Evan only has eyes for me.

The picture I'd seen of his eyes, it didn't do them justice. The pale jade visibly brightens as he looks at me. The green brings out the spattering of brown freckles against his nose, the light nutmeg color of his skin. The long brown curls falling just slightly in his face.

Those eyes are undeniably the most beautiful eyes I've ever seen. I scan every bit of his face and it's only when the corners of his eyes crinkle as he smiles, that I realize he's doing the same to me. At his smile I release a breath I hadn't realized I was holding.

The way he smiles, it's like I'm the sun peeking through gray clouds. There is such open love and trust in that look. His entire face is a part of that smile. He is far more attractive in this moment than all the other times I've visited. I'm not even sure if being awake is the difference. It's his smile.

I'd worried that Evan might be angry at me upon waking up, or at least aggravated, but the way he's looking at me now, with a mixture of relief and utter happiness, I realize that all my worries were wrong. I barely notice someone shuffling by me.

I'm not sure how long I stand in the doorway with my feet frozen in place. I'm vaguely aware of more people shuffling by me, a pat on my back.

My eyes are locked with Evan's, but then he lifts his arms just a little off the bed. He holds them open as if waiting for a hug and I'm propelled forward.

I didn't realize how much I needed him to be okay. Even though I don't remember him, I can feel my body relaxing, as if I haven't breathed a true sigh of relief in months. That hug is like the first breath of air a drowning man takes upon being rescued. Painful, sweet, and the most marvelous thing.

And I'm crying, from relief, from the released tension, the built-up fear, everything. Even when I realized I'd lost my memories, I didn't cry. But now it's like a broken faucet and I can't stop. I'm not even sure at this point if I'm crying for myself or him. I have no memories and who knows how broken he might be.

It should be me comforting him, but he just pulls me into the hug, rubs soothing circles on my back. Neither one of us say anything at first, as if we're afraid to break the silence.

I lay in the little hospital bed next to him for what feels like eons, and when I'm finally finished crying I tell him about everything. The amnesia, the accident, my investigation, Hei and Mimi, Carren, Analise, meeting Risa, anything I can think of. He listens, meeting my gaze the entire time.

It's only when Cadence and Harp are back in the room talking about their own things that

I finally move away from him, but I don't get off the bed and I don't let go of his hand. I need that connection more than anything. He's awake. He's alive. Someone that knows everything about that night. Even if it turns out he doesn't remember, it'll be okay, because I'm not the only survivor now. And whatever happened... whatever will happen, I'm not alone anymore.

Evan never says a word the entire time we talk to him, but he smiles and laughs and listens. I keep a hold of his hand as a tether to reality. He's back but something must be wrong, because there's an Evan sitting beside me, and another one standing at the door.

Chapter 19

'*Quick, quick, lock the doors.*' I dive into the backseat of the car. Someone fumbles with a key in the driver's seat.

'*Do you see anything?*'

'*Start the car already!*' A girl in the passenger seat is crying. The driver manages to get the keys in the ignition, but the engine just turns over.

'*It's not starting!*'

'*Try again!*' The girl is screaming now.

The person next to me reaches over to pull my seatbelt on. The engine turns again. There's a sudden screeching of metal on metal and the whole car is shaking.

A hand latches on to mine. In front of us the driver and passenger exchange a look, reach for one another's hands. The car is moving, but we aren't moving it.

'*We're going to die.*' The girl cries.

The driver cracks a joke and she laughs, almost hysterically.

'*I love you guys, if this is how we go, I'm okay with that. If any of us makes it, you tell my mom—*'

I wake up with a start, my heart pounding in my ears. I shake the lingering bits of nightmare out of my mind and glance at the clock. It's three in the morning; I roll over with a sigh but then decide to go get a snack.

Serenity is in the kitchen when I arrive.

"Can't sleep, Pumpkin?" She asks.

"I had a... umm I think it might have been a dream of the accident?" Bits and pieces come back to me.

Darryl and Margaret in the front seats, Evan holding my hand, but I can't make sense of the screeching metal on metal, and how was the car moving on its own? Maybe it's not actually a memory and just a nightmare created by my subconscious?

"Do you want to talk about it?" I see she's got a book in front of her and what looks like a mug of warm milk.

I shake my head and pull the milk from the fridge.

"Making cocoa?" Serenity asks, as she steps up to pull a small pot from the cabinet. "Let me?" Even though she's asking she's already pulling cocoa, sugar, and vanilla from the pantry. It's clear she wants to. I cede the control to her and take a seat at the table, watching as she begins heating the milk.

"Homemade cocoa was always the way we put you back to bed, you know. Even if you don't remember, you're still the same."

She gives me one of those sad but loving smiles. We're quiet for a time as she whisks cocoa and sugar into the milk. She leaves it to heat and pulls butterscotch cookies from the cabinet. I munch on one of the cookies as I watch her.

"Everyone went to visit Evan, I know Cadence and I were friends with him, but he was really close to everyone, wasn't he?" She gives me a side-glance with a little smirk. This is the first time in months that I've asked her a question and if she's surprised, then she isn't showing it.

"You could say something like that. Evan's been close to you and the boys for about five... six years now? It's been long enough that it's almost hard not to remember a time when he wasn't around. It's been quiet without him being over for dinner."

"He used to come over for dinner?" I know he did since Cadence mentioned it before after Mama Etta had stopped in for the third time. But I'm grasping for things to talk about.

"Every Thursday, Friday, and Saturday. Thursday's are Mama Etta's poker night, Friday nights she goes dancing, and Saturdays her bowling league meets. She sometimes would come over on Wednesdays for dinner and to Sunday breakfast." Serenity turns the heat down on the stove and starts whisking the cocoa to make it frothy.

"We should probably have her over again soon." She says after a moment.

It doesn't even surprise me that Mama Etta has an active social life. In fact, if Serenity had said she liked to ride a motorcycle and go skydiving in her spare time, I wouldn't have even questioned it. And I'd love to see her playing poker, I bet it's entertaining.

Finished whisking, Serenity ladles two mugs with the cocoa and tops them with marshmallows and whip cream and drizzles a little caramel sauce over the top. She passes one to me and sits back down with her own.

"You and Evan spent practically all your spare time chasing adventures together you know. I'm sure they've told you that already. You went hiking, on scavenger hunts, skating. The boys often joined in of course."

"They mentioned some of it." I say.

"Evan is practically a part of the family now. He and Mama Etta. He's even gone on vacation with us, and he and Mama Etta have spent the last few years' worth of holidays with our family as well." She's still smirking, as if she has a secret.

Serenity starts telling me stories of some of the craziest things we did. The top of her list and one of the most recent is a paint fight that crept into the house, leaving colored footprints everywhere. Luckily the paint was easily washed out, but we'd been covered in brown from where all the colors had mixed together. And we'd had to clean the kitchen and parts of the living room carpet.

"You had to throw away that swimsuit; you couldn't get the paint out." She says with a laugh. She glances behind me at the microwave clock. "It's nearly five now, you should head back to bed, Pumpkin."

Settling back into bed with my mug of cocoa, it doesn't take long to fall back asleep.

Chapter 20

My night or rather my morning is filled with more nightmares, the sound of crunching metal and Margaret's cries. I don't know if the nightmares are memories, but I have a feeling they might be.

It's almost like Evan waking up has facilitated my own recovery. The nightmares leave me drenched in sweat and after the fifth time waking up in a panic I give up on sleep altogether. I'm relieved when Cadence bursts into my room sometime in the afternoon.

"We have to get to the hospital. Now."

I try to shake away the remnants of the last nightmare. Cadence is pulling clothes from my closet and throwing them at me.

"Get dressed. Something happened."

"Evan?" The look he gives me sends shivers down my spine.

"I-I don't... I don't know. Mama Etta just called... hurry, Clef's driving."

I rush to get ready, panic making my movements sloppier. I have to search for pants since Cadence threw five shirts at me for some reason. It takes four tries to get my shirt buttoned properly.

Evan *has* to be okay. He just woke up. He *has* to be fine. We haven't even talked yet. He's got to be okay.

The ride to the hospital, crammed in the backseat between Harp and Cadence is tense. No one knows what to say, and even if I could get my mouth to form the words, I'm not sure that anything I say could make this situation any better. I feel numb as I follow my brothers into the hospital. Mama Etta is waiting in one of the waiting rooms along with our parents. Their heads bowed together, faces strained.

"What happened?" Cadence asks. He seems to be taking this the hardest of all of us. Every inch of him is tense, his face filled with absolute terror. He couldn't sit still in the car the entire way here, as if he needed to be moving.

"Sit down sweetie," Mama Etta says. Cadence does but he bounces his legs up and down and taps rhythms on his knees. The rest of us take our seats a little slower.

The section of the waiting room we're in is relatively empty. There's a few anxious looking people and what looks like another family asleep in a few of the chairs. The TV is a silent hum of some home improvement show. There's a little coffee station set up in the corner, definitely need a little of that right now.

"Mama Etta thought we might want to be here..." Serenity says in a tight voice. She leaves the statement hanging but we all know what she's implying.

"He's still being treated; we're not really sure exactly *what* happened. I got a call early this morning." Mama Etta is calm, but I can

189

tell by the way she clenches her cane in her fists that she's worried. Her green hair isn't even styled.

"They said there had been some sort of incident. He pressed the call button and when the nurses came in the room he'd yanked his IV out. At first, they thought he was having some sort of fit. They warned that he could have hallucinations and might have fits after he woke up, but he managed to tell them..." She glances over at me now. "He said someone put something in the IV. That it didn't look like a nurse. He kept insisting they check it."

Someone tried to kill him. The thought makes me suck in a breath as Mama Etta continues. I could be wrong. Maybe I'm jumping to conclusions. But if it really was a nurse then Evan wouldn't have freaked out so much, right? But what if he was hallucinating?

"They checked his vitals to calm him down. And they found an excessive amount of potassium in his system. Hyperkalemia is what they called it. They're treating him now but...." She leaves that hanging as well.

No one wants to say what might happen. Serenity starts talking about her latest song or something. I can tell she's only trying to provide a distraction for everyone. Cadence gets up and starts pacing back and forth and Clef goes over to the coffee station and begins pouring cups for everyone.

"Have you contacted the police?" I ask. Everyone turns to stare at me like I've turned a different color or something. "He wasn't hallucinating, right?"

"Pumpkin, he could've been, we're just lucky that the hallucination helped them find out what was wrong before it got worse."

Serenity pats me on the shoulder. I glance over at Cadence who stops pacing long enough to arch a brow at me. I can tell he's thinking the same thing as me, but how can we convince everyone? Especially when I don't have any real proof... I doubt the cops would listen to a teenager's gut instinct. But I'm certain.

It's just too coincidental that the day after it's announced in the paper that Evan woke up, something happens to him. Someone tried to kill him and whoever it was, I bet they had something to do with Jeanette's disappearance.

Chapter 21

"I should never have let you talk me into coming back here." Cadence says as he peers at one of the no trespassing signs.

"I told you about the nightmares, right? I have a theory I want to test." Cadence let's out a long sigh but follows me as I walk up and down the fence line. I can't see much past the chain links, just a few piles of gravel and other various construction tools. For a moment I think I hear the sound of a machine.

Everything goes black for a second, a flashlight glaring on the metal links. I shake away the edging darkness and continue examining the fence. It's the middle of the day, there's not even a hint of clouds.

The fence itself isn't actually that tall and there's no barbed wire at the top, which gets me thinking. I glance up and down as far as I can see. There are no signs warning against electrocution, just the no trespassing signs. With the whole area being a construction zone, it isn't too busy up here.

"Hey Cadence, keep lookout for a moment." I say.

"Lookout for wha—" Cadence lets out a noise that sounds like a cross between a screeching tire and an underwater gurgle.

"Are you insane?"

The answer is probably yes. After all I've been hearing voices, seeing things, and I'm fairly certain I'm having nightmares that may or may not be memories. And now I'm about to trespass because I'm sure that Jeanette Water's disappearance has something to do with this construction site. I have no idea how to explain why I think this, but it's almost a compulsion to see whatever this is to the end.

"Lyric Lysanne Lyons! Get back down here!" Cadence yells, he reaches to pull me from the fence but I'm already pulling myself over the top.

"Just yell if you see any cars or anything and I'll hide, give me ten minutes, okay." I tell him as I drop down on the other side. Cadence's face is red, and he looks like he's about to climb up the fence too.

"Keep a lookout, I'll be right back. I just want to look around for a moment." Cadence clenches his teeth and takes a step up the fence.

"Beats, trust me." He stops and stares at me for a moment.

"Not fair, using that." He grumbles. After a long pause he nods and let's go of the fence.

Inside the construction site is about what you'd expect, except tools are just lying everywhere as if they were forgotten about.

It looks like only half of the foundation is finished. There's metal frames and piles of rubble. The claw machine catches my eye, I can't quite tell from where I'm at, but it almost looks like there's blue paint marks on the orangish metal.

There's a few scraps of trash and the sound of a cup moving in the wind makes me jump.

I think I hear another noise and then I hear what I was waiting for.

My voice.

"Did you hear that? Why would a machine be on at night?"

"We should go, this was a bad idea. You should just tell Clef what you know." One of the guys voices.

"They must be working still, it's not like it's that late after all." The other guy's voice.

"Wait, shhh, do you see that?" Margaret.

I glance around as if trying to see what they saw, and I think I glimpse it for a moment, everything darkens, there's the sound of something pouring.

"Lyric your ten minutes are up, get back here now!" Cadence shouts through the fence.

Everything returns to normal slowly, like coming up for air after jumping into a pool. I examine the concrete and machines one last time, trying to read clues in the unfinished foundation and tools, before making my way back. Cadence is almost to the top of the fence when I reach it.

I laugh for a good few minutes before I can climb back over. He just scowls at me.

"Stop that, you were taking too long. We should go."

"Sooo... did you find what you were looking for?" Cadence asks. He's trying for a casual tone, but I can tell from how tense he is that he's holding back a barrage of questions.

"I don't know. I think— that night, I think I was in there."

"But... do you remember why?"

"No... I'm not sure, but I think it connects with Jeanette's disappearance. I just don't know why. Call it a hunch?"

He purses his lips, "I've never been one to question your instincts. You have an uncanny habit of picking up on things others don't. You once figured out where Dad left his keys because of a candy bar wrapper."

"Well, my instincts are telling me that the disappearance of Jeanette has something to with the accident, and... I think I... well I didn't quite remember, but everything there," I pause trying to think of the best way to say this without sounding crazy. "It felt familiar, like I'd been there before, and it makes sense. The place where the car crashed isn't too far from here." Cadence nods and goes silent, as if mulling over what I've told him.

I'm trying to think of what our next course of action should be when his phone rings.

Chapter 22

As we come into the hospital, I see a glimpse of the familiar curly locks of Jeanette Waters. I stop and turn to watch and it's almost like everything around me stops. I'm vaguely aware of Cadence asking me what's wrong. Of people milling out of the hospital.

Jeanette and Wright are huddled to the side of the entryway. Almost hidden by a shrub. This looks a little like the picture that was in the paper. She's waving her hands angrily. He's stoic, a pinch of humor in his gaze. Finally, he nods, and she seems to calm. I can almost read the relief in her face. They walk off, going in different directions and I blink to see Cadence in my face.

"What happened?" He asks.

It dawns on me then. I'm not going crazy.

At least not completely.

"Memory... they're memories."

"Lyric?" Cadence's voice drips worry.

"I'm... seeing... *memory!*" I laugh out of relief. All the moments with Evan, the things I was hearing.

Memories, that would explain why Evan's ghost didn't disappear when he woke up. Why the séance didn't work. Why he would never talk to me. It was never a ghost to begin with.

I think back on what I just saw. It must've been just a brief interaction. I probably just noticed it in passing and didn't even think of it until she went missing. I must've recognized the woman. That must be how Wright connects to all this. The picture in the paper wasn't clear enough but now I can definitely tell that they weren't lovers. Something else was going on. If I'd remembered this before and then found out about his relationship to Cole, then perhaps that was why we were at that construction site.

"You're seeing what now?"

"I'll explain later. We should go see Evan while we have a chance." He gives me a dubious look but follows me into the hospital to Evan's room.

Evan is sitting up, a plate with a turkey sandwich and some fruit and pudding in front of him. Without thinking I snatch a strawberry from the plate and plop down on the bed, while Cadence takes the chair. I start to stand when I realize what I've done but Evan laughs and pulls me back down, handing me another strawberry.

"Good to see you awake again. You really need to stop with the near-death moments, I can only handle so much stress, you know." Cadence says. He passes Evan a bag filled with junk food that we stopped to pick up on the way.

"So, tell us about the person that tried to kill you." I ask. Cadence gapes at me.

"Lyric... what, don't just lead with that!"

197

We'd discussed in the car what we would ask him about. As much I wanted to start with the questions about why we were at the construction site and if he remembered what happened, the most prevalent thing is to find out who hurt him and then go from there. The past can wait until he's out of danger.

Evan blinks at us for a moment.

"No one else believed me." He says after a moment. He talks slowly, carefully as if it takes effort for every word. His voice is raspy, but I can tell that when it's normal it would be beautiful. "They said that I was hallucinating."

"I don't think so. We were involved in something that caused our accident, weren't we?" He nods.

"Guy, normal looking. Wasn't wearing scrubs. Didn't act like a nurse. He kept... looking over his shoulder. Thought I was asleep. Average height. Black hair."

"Well, that could be practically anyone. Did he say anything?" Cadence asks.

Evan shakes his head again. He pushes the rest of his food towards us. His eyes are starting to droop a little.

"The accident...." I start. I'm afraid of what he will tell me. He gives my hand a squeeze as if telling me it's okay to go on. "What do you remember?" I ask, keeping the question simple.

"You thought that she might be there. Had to do with Analise. You and Margaret."

"She. Jeanette, right? We were trying to find where she was?" I exchange a look with Cadence.

"Found her." Evan says. Before I can ask more, a nurse comes in to check on him and by the time she's finished Evan is sleeping again.

The rest of our questions will have to wait, I guess.

Chapter 23

"Found her." I repeat for the tenth time as Cadence holds the front door for me. It seems we're the only one's home. Godzilla comes running and I leave the door open long enough for him to go outside and come back. I follow Cadence to his room, the words echoing in my head. "We found her."

"He was starting to fall asleep, Leary. Maybe he wasn't saying what you think he was saying."

"Don't you dare start. Someone tried to *kill* him. That wasn't a hallucination. I don't believe that for a second. We found her. She must've been at the site. She had to be, and someone tried to run us off and we wrecked. But I don't understand how Analise and Margaret fit in." Cadence visibly pales.

"I don't like where you're going with this." He says. "How did you know she was at that site?" I think back to my earlier flashback.

"If I tell you a crazy theory, do you promise not to have me committed?" I ask.

Cadence glances over and raises both his eyebrows. I think he's trying to arch just one, but it's not working. He plops onto his desk chair and swivels around to watch me. Perdita, hidden beneath the desk, jumps on his lap and starts headbutting him for scratches.

I start the theory slowly. Explaining how I thought I was seeing Evan's ghost for the past few months.

"And you didn't say anything?"

"I thought I was crazy, or maybe something about my near-death experience caused me to see ghosts. That theory didn't last since it was only ever Evan that I saw." I take a breath before saying the next part. "And you all were strangers. I didn't know how to broach the subject."

"So, are you still seeing him, and uh... hearing things?" Cadence asks, not a hint of judgement in his voice. I let out a sigh of relief.

"Yes, not nearly as much now, but I'm seeing other things. I think I'm seeing my memories. Like maybe they're really vivid flashbacks."

"That's what you meant." Cadence says.

"I saw a scene of the janitor and Jeanette. They're body language didn't say lovers. She was agitated about something."

"You think the janitor did something?"

"I don't know. There's pieces we're still missing, I think. Other than what I saw, they didn't seem to have any connection to one another. No one even mentioned that the two of them knew each other."

"You think Analise knew anything? Maybe she was the reason you made the connection?" Cadence asks.

"You said I was good at connecting puzzles, if she'd made even a casual comment about the two of them then I would've picked up on it, right? And Evan did mention her."

He nods. Cadence turns to his computer and opens a Word document.

"List the facts," He says.

"Jeanette was last seen at the hospital." I start. "The janitor, Wright, could easily have been one of the last people around her."

"And Wright is going to be inheriting Desmond Cole's estate, part of which is the construction site the car accident happened near." Cadence adds.

"The person I talked with, they said it was sudden. He'd been doing better when he took a turn for the worse and died."

"He died of a stroke, right?" Cadence asks, pausing in his typing.

"He was old though, and he was already in the hospital for something..." Before I can tell Cadence to look it up, he's already searching.

"Local business tycoon, Desmond Cole has postponed plans for new mall due to possible cancer." Cadence starts reading aloud. How did I miss that when I was researching him? I peer over Cadence's shoulder at the date. Cadence clicks over to another tab and types in the words Desmond Cole and Cancer.

"Plans for the new mall will soon be underway, says a spokesperson of Cole Industries. Desmond Cole is set to be released in less than a week after receiving news that he is cancer free." Cadence reads again. "He was in the hospital to get a tumor removed and they discovered it wasn't cancerous, but he still died."

"He died of a stroke... the patient Jeanette lost died of a stroke."

"Two elderly patients in a hospital dying of strokes. Not really that suspicious."

"But the dates are close, and Cole was supposed to be released. I'm assuming they would've already found out if he had any heart problems, right?" Cadence is typing away.

"What are you looking for?"

"You remember what Mama Etta said about Evan's attack. Hyperkalemia. Look here. Severe potassium overdose that can lead to cardiac arrest." Cadence reads. "You believe what he said about being attacked. What if all the strokes connect?"

"But that still wouldn't explain the connection between Jeanette and Wright."

"I think we need to talk to Analise again." I say with a sigh.

Before Cadence can answer we hear the sound of steps running on the stairs, meaning Harp is home, and probably everyone else. And the last time I talked with Analise I basically told her off, I doubt she'll be forthcoming with information now.

After listing all the facts several times we'd stay up late into the night researching everything we already know, trying to find any missing pieces to connect everything. All it gets us is little sleep and a late start into the day.

Chapter 24

When we finally get up Cadence is grumbly as he takes me to the hospital to visit Evan. He can't stay with me because of the thing he's been hiding from me. I still need to talk to him about that. From my journal entries I'm starting to think it had something to do with school, but I'm not sure.

We haven't decided on how to confront Analise yet. Cadence thinks we should wait to see if anything else happens first, or if I have any more flashes. I disagree but after we talked about it more, there's not really anything else we can do.

It's not like we can go to the police. We have a bunch of facts and barely a connection, plus there's no evidence to prove what we think. So, we're just going to make sure Evan doesn't have much time by himself for the next few days until we decide how best to confront Analise.

"You sure you want to hang out here all day? Clef doesn't get off until dinnertime." He reminds me for the fifteenth time. "I can come back when I'm finished."

I honestly think he's just a little jealous that I'm going to get to spend some time with awake Evan and he isn't.

Although he *could* insist on coming back, I think he wants to give Evan and me some time with one another. But I don't want to call him out on it.

"Yes, I'll be fine. It's not even that long. Besides we both agreed that someone should try to stay with him," I swallow, "just in case."

He shoots me a look.

"It's nearly five hours... and I know. I'm just worried." He runs a hand through his bedhead. "About both of you."

"We'll be fine, and Clef will be around. Nothing will happen in bright daylight, I'm sure of it. Besides I'll have good company and the murder mystery book you recommended, and that other book that you and Risa liked. And I want to ask Evan more about what he said." Cadence let's out a groan.

"I wish you'd tell me what it is that's so important that you can't stay." I say.

"Eventually." With that he goes quiet, a comfortable blanket of stillness falling over the car. "Tell Evan I'll come by tomorrow."

"Hey, you know whatever you're hiding, I won't hold it against you." He gives me a side grin and rolls his eyes.

"I don't think you could hold anything against me. You know I'm your favorite."
Now it's my turn to roll my eyes, even if he can't see me.

"Pretty certain that *I'm* my favorite."

"You could at least play along," He says with a fake hurt tone.

We lapse into a comfortable silence again until he comes to the hospital entrance.

"Don't forget to let Clef know that you're going back home with him." Cadence reminds me as I hop out. I wave his concerns away and rush off to Evan's room.

Evan's watching cartoons when I knock.

"Hey, how are you feeling today? You were in and out of sleep yesterday."

He grins sheepishly at me and I slowly make my way to the bed.

I pull out a bag of sunflower seeds and a tangerine.

"Cadence said these were your favorites. He wasn't messing with me, right?"

Evan let's out a hoarse chuckle and motions for me to place them with all the other assortments of goodies, the majority is from my family. They're all practically overflowing off the counter now. There is one basket with a tag that says it's from Mrs. Davies.

The most surprising is a vase of blue and white flowers with The Rising Eclipse on the tag. A smaller vase of daffodils next to it is from Hei and Mimi. I'd texted them as soon as Evan woke up, and they said they'd try to visit sometime next week. It's nice to see they sent something. I manage to find a little space between one of the baskets and the stuffed bumblebee.

"You look tired." He says as I settle in the chair next to him.

"Yeah, I haven't had a few months' worth of sleep," I say before realizing how that sounds, but Evan is laughing. "Just a late night. Researching. You... uh..." I gulp.

The steady beep of the machines has never seemed so loud. "We don't have to talk about the accident first. I mean... I would be lying if I said I didn't want to talk about it, but we don't have to start with it. I'm sure there are much better things to start with. I... why don't we start... um..."

He's staring at me so intensely it's making me nervous. Like those jade eyes can read my every thought.

"What's your favorite color?" I blurt and then sort of stare, almost horrified.

It was so much easier when this was a one-sided thing. He might remember me, but with the exception of my venting sessions, I don't remember a thing about him. We're practically strangers.

Evan laughs, maybe at the question, maybe at my expression, I'm not really sure.

"Same as you." He says after he finally stops laughing.

I think about all the yellow in my room. How I've hated the color for the past few months, how the cheeriness has steadily annoyed me, especially how the color seemed to suit the *me* before, but not the *me* now.

"I'm not really sure I like yellow anymore. It's just so... out there." I expect him to look disappointed, or to give me that look everyone else does. That pitying look. Instead, he smiles.

"You know when we were first trying to become friends I blurted that question out too." He speaks so slowly as if every word requires a lot of energy to get out. "When you said yellow I asked you if it was because it reminded you of sunshine and you said no." He turns to give me another bright smile.

"Then why did I like it?"

"Yellow, it's the brightest color and it's one of the most noticeable. There's a reason they make reflective vests and signs out of it, you know. It's not always appreciated, but it always stands out. And you said you wanted to be like that. You said that just like the sun always rises, yellow is still bright, even when it starts to fade."

Chapter 25

I wake up to something smothering me. I don't remember when I fell asleep. The beeping of machines reminds me I'm still in the hospital. I blearily recall moving to sit beside Evan in the bed and playing twenty questions. Analise. He told me the connection. I need to tell Cadence.

Evan's breathing is even beside me, but I can't quite tell if he's asleep or just being quiet. The sound of an infomercial distracts me. I wonder how long I've been asleep. I notice the shuffling sound of footsteps, the kind that indicate someone trying not to be too loud.

I move to pull the blanket off me when Evan squeezes down, keeping them over my head. At first, I think that it's probably Cadence, or even Clef that Evan wants to try to scare, but then I hear a muttered voice.

"I tried to make this easy." It's a smooth male voice. I suck in a breath as my adrenaline spikes. I don't recognize this voice. The footsteps slide closer. Evan gives me another squeeze, as if in warning. I don't know if it's the adrenaline or something else but suddenly I'm not staring through the scratchy white blanket anymore.

'Quick, quick, lock the doors.' I dive into the backseat of the car. Darryl is fumbling with keys in the driver's seat.

'Do you see anything?' He asks.

'Start the car already!' Margaret cries from the passenger seat. Her eyes are brimming with tears but anger simmers below the surface. Darryl manages to get the keys in the ignition, but the engine just turns over.

'It's not starting!'

'Try again!' Margaret screams.

Evan reaches over, and I hear the click of my seatbelt as he buckles it. The engine turns again. There's a sudden screeching of metal on metal and the whole car is shaking.

Evan's hand latches on to mine. In front of us Margaret and Darryl exchange a look, reach for one another's hands. The car is moving, but we aren't moving it.

Outside of the window we can see the ground getting smaller, the car is airborne.

'We're going to die.' Margaret says.

Darryl cracks a corny joke and she laughs, almost hysterically.

'I love you guys," Darryl says as the car sways. He makes eye contact with all of us. 'If this is how we go, I'm okay with that. If any of us makes it, you tell my mom how much I love her, and about the letter, okay. Make sure she reads it.'

He turns to Margaret and I look away as they kiss. I turn to Evan to say something but then the car is falling. More than one someone is screaming. I think I'm one of them. The impact happens in almost slow motion. Jarring metal. The car rolling over and over. Near blinding pain. Broken. Something is broken.

When the car finally stops moving it feels like hours have passed. Something is smoking. There's a heavy ringing in my ears. Blood is dripping into my eyes. Evan's hand has fallen away. My face is numb. I battle with the seatbelt. My door is practically caved in. The only reason I'm not crushed is because I was sitting in the middle.

'Evan, Darryl, Margaret?' I call. My voice sounds strange in my own ears, like it's really far away. Everyone is slumped over.

Margaret and Darryl are covered in blood. So much blood. I gag, feeling my stomach rebelling. I swallow down bile. The smell of smoke drifts in and I fight to move my limbs. Sharp pain shoots behind my eyes. I need to get out of the car. Need to get out. I crawl over Evan and kick the door open. I drag him out and go back.

I think the car might be on fire. Need to get everyone away. Need to get them out. The ringing in my ears hasn't stopped. The smell of gas hits me. There might be a leak somewhere.

My vision is going in and out. It takes every ounce of strength I have to pull Darryl and Margaret from the car. To drag all three of them away. Black creeps at the edges of everything.

None of them stir, and I can feel my limbs starting to get shaky as my adrenaline wears off. They look so broken, but Margaret is the worse. Her right side is all odd angles, I think

I can see bone. There's so much blood everywhere, in my eyes, on them.

The car really is on fire.

Phone. I need to call someone. My limbs feel like ice.

My phone is still in the car, so I crawl to Evan and search his pockets, call 911.

I barely register the voice on the other end questioning me.

'Car, fire, help.' I say before everything finally goes black.

Chapter 26

The hospital room comes back to me slower than the other times I had a flashback. The accident. I remember the accident. I don't remember what we saw, why we were running, or anything else, but I remember the crash.

Tears prick at my eyes as the terror floods through my limbs. Adrenaline courses through me. It takes a conscious effort to calm myself down. It felt so real. As if it was happening again.

I'm not in the car anymore.

I'm alive.

Evan's awake.

We're not in the car anymore.

I'm not bleeding.

We're alive. I can feel the tension slowly easing the more things I repeat to myself.

I stifle a gasp as details fall into place.

The crane machine at the construction site, the paint on the claw makes sense now. The railing that looked like it was never touched.

The blanket is suddenly pulled away and I grasp for it at the same time as Evan. The muttering voice stairs at me now, in his hands is a pillow.

Wayne Charles Wright is just as bland as his photo made him out to be. What Analise saw in him is definitely not looks. Then again, I have a feeling Analise knew he was related to Cole all along.

My journal neglected to say that one of my schemes worked and Margaret and I caught the two of them together. We confronted her about it and Evan said we threatened her, telling her to tell Clef or we would.

That wasn't too long before the accident. She'd come clean to us that Clef was really a ploy to make Wright jealous because she thought he was secretly seeing Jeanette. A ploy that didn't work. I'm guessing she thought she was in the clear after the accident since Clef didn't discover her affair until afterwards.

Wright clenches his fist around the fabric of the pillow. He hadn't planned on someone being here, obviously. His eyes dart from me to Evan, trying to determine who to attack first, I think.

"You killed her that night. Didn't you?" I ask, trying to keep his attention on me. I just hope Evan's taking this chance to call the nurses. I fumble with my phone in my pocket, trying to call someone. I type a message first, hoping that it makes sense.

Wright doesn't respond to me but takes a calculated step towards Evan, his eyes narrowing.

"You buried her in the cement, right? Why, though? She had nothing to do with you, right?"

I remember Cadence pointing out that the same thing that almost killed Evan could be the reason for Desmond Cole's stroke.

"She saw you kill your Uncle, right? You wanted to keep her from talking, maybe you couldn't buy her silence?"

That gets a startled laugh out of him.

"You've got the right ideas kid, but you're on the wrong track. I didn't kill him. She did."

I dart a glance to Evan to see him pressing the nurses button.

That moment of distraction costs me. Before I even notice him moving, Wright is lunging around the bed and pulling me into a choke hold. Evan drops the call remote and his eyes widen in panic.

"Tell them you pressed it by accident." Wright whispers. His arm presses into my trachea a bit and I reach up to try to pull the arm away.

An intercom goes off as a nurse asks if there's anything we need.

"Umm, sorry I-uh, rolled over in my sleep. Accident." Evan mutters. I don't pay attention to the nurse's response. Wright backs up, pulling me with him and thankfully loosens his hold enough for me to breathe again.

"Why would she kill him?" I ask, still trying to distract him. I can tell he's floundering. He's trying to figure out how to walk out of here without us saying something or getting caught. Evan is shaking his head at me, as if telling me to be quiet, but the longer he stays here, the better our chances of getting out of this. And what Evan doesn't know is that I remember something that will help us both.

"At first, I got the job here just to reconnect with him, you know. My dear *rich* uncle. I was his only living relative after all. But it turns out the old man had a daughter." He responds, much to my surprise. "He was planning on reconnecting with her after he got out of here. His nearly having cancer gave him an epiphany or something. He had his will rewritten and was leaving her everything. I didn't plan to kill him, however when opportunity presents itself," he punctuates this with another step towards the door. "It's almost a crime not to take it."

"You blackmailed her somehow, right?" I ask. Evan is mouthing for me to stop talking.

"Call it a moment of serendipity. I saw her one night with an older patient. The woman was wasting away, and she put her out of her misery. I threatened to tell someone."

I can piece it together now. The widow's death that bothered Jeanette so bad. It wasn't that it was a patient that died or that she'd been there to witness the death, it was that she'd killed her.

"So, you killed her. Tying up loose ends?" I give Evan a wink to let him know I'm needling the guy. And I can see him relax a little, as if he knows what I'm planning. He trusts me.

"I didn't plan to, but her conscious was eating away at her. She was breaking." He squeezes my neck a little more and I sputter. "I couldn't have her telling anyone."

"And then you tried to kill us when we saw you that night. You figured you'd bury her in the cement and by happenstance we were there that night," I'm speculating now because I don't actually remember that part, but the sounds I remembered would make sense. "Since you were going to inherit it anyway, no one would notice, right? And it was perfect. No one would even suspect you of killing him since everyone thought it was natural causes."

"But she was going to *ruin* it, and you kids decided to get involved. I don't know how you found out the connection, but you won't live long enough to tell anyone." Hmm... so he doesn't know that Analise is the connection. At least that means, hopefully, that she had no idea what he'd planned. She just knew he was rich and wanted him.

He starts to squeeze my neck again, lifting me almost off my feet, but this time I grab at his elbow and my body reacts without much effort. I've done this before, with my brothers, after all. All the times I've practiced this move with Alto, Harp, Cadence, Clef, and even Evan and Darryl, come back to me.

I throw my weight down and sweep to the side, so that my legs are behind his, and yank my head out of his arms. Using my grip on his elbow and grabbing his hand, I pin his arm behind him, forcing him to his knees.

His other arm flails out to try to stop me and I bend his hand back to the point of nearly breaking it.

I press my knees into his back and look over at Evan who has a smug grin.

"Still badass, I see."

I laugh as I remember a particular time I was teaching Evan the same move I just used.

"Oh, hush and call the nurses, will you?"

Chapter 27

It seemed almost anticlimactic to watch hospital security escort Wright out. It was nearly 1:00 in the morning by that point.

The blanket Evan had covered me with had been enough for no one to even realize I was still in the room.

I'd forgotten to tell Clef I was in the hospital and I'd been asleep far past his shift. Someone had called in, and he was pulling a double, and had no idea where I was. Cadence was just about to come back to see what I was doing when I'd texted him.

I'd managed to leave most of my conversation with Wright as a voicemail on Cadence's phone, thankfully the typed message I wrote without looking, telling him not to answer, made enough sense that he didn't, meaning the police could have a partially taped confession. I told the police such when they came to get our statements.

The officer had grunted a little about us nosing into an investigation, but I think it was partly to hide that she was actually rather impressed.

When everything hit the news, Analise came forward to testify against Wright. I'm not sure if her conscious plagued her, or if it was for the attention or even revenge, but she played the frightened witness well.

She hadn't actually known that Wright had killed Cole, but she knew enough about his meetings with Jeanette to provide evidence against him. And she'd known where he was that night, it's the reason we knew where to go. She'd been tracking his phone. We *had* gone there to find Jeanette that night, but we hadn't realized how we'd find her.

After Margaret and I had confronted Analise, she'd turned the situation around on us. We had been searching for Jeanette after all and her farfetched thoughts was that the two were lovers planning on running away together as soon as Wright claimed his inheritance. She agreed to break up and leave Clef alone if I told her whether Wright was really seeing Jeanette or not. I was right that she was lying about that part.

The biggest evidence against Wright was at the construction site. Jeanette Waters' body was uncovered under the cement and there was enough DNA evidence to link him to the crime scene.

Wright was being charged with first-degree murder and voluntary manslaughter. He was most likely going to live the rest of his years in jail.

Evan had to wait a few more weeks, undergoing more tests and beginning therapy, before he was released from the hospital. He still had his memories, unlike me, but the coma made it harder for him to talk and remember things quickly. It hadn't just been my imagination that he was speaking slowly.

The months in bed had also left his muscles weaker. And they were worried about an injury to his spine that might keep him from walking. But hopefully, with enough physical therapy, he could get better. Until then we were all going to support him as much as we could.

My late night in the hospital resulted in one other good thing besides catching the bad guy. I'm not sure when they started talking, perhaps at some point while the police were getting statements, but Bridget and Clef hit it off. I don't know if it'll go anywhere but I'm rooting for anything that'll make him happy and she does seem to be a genuinely nice person. She was one of the first to make it to the room after Evan called for help and insisted on examining me and Evan both for injuries.

Not all my memories are back. Carren said that I should continue as I have been and not rush it, they'll come when they're ready. I'm still not quite the same as before, but I'm learning not to worry so much about that.

My family still give me those looks, but I'm working on not feeling so guilty about it. I finally mentioned it to Carren and she said to remember that they mean well, that no matter what, they still love me.

She's right. I can see it a little better now that I'm not wallowing in guilt. I see it in the moments when Reid knocks on my bedroom door with snacks or just to check on me. When Alto tells me a joke and Cadence makes me tea. When Serenity cooks and bakes for me. When Clef will just sit and talk. When Harp wakes me up early to run. They're learning they didn't lose me... just as I'm learning me.

I still see the ghost, or rather the *memory* of Evan and sometimes other realistic flashbacks but other than Cadence, I haven't told anyone else. I think I might tell Evan about it one day. If anyone would understand, it's probably him.

As for Desmond Cole's inheritance. It seemed that his secret heir was closer than any of us had realized...

* * *

"So, this, this letter... I can't believe it." Mrs. Davies practically collapses on her leather green couch, tears flooding her eyes. "How... how did he?"

Apparently, the letter had arrived addressed to all of the Davies'. The date was just a few days before Cole's death. Around the same date of my first journal entry mentioning an investigation.

Evan tells her how Darryl had opened it first and then hid it from her. Darryl had wanted to investigate the validity of it, but before he could talk to Desmond Cole, he died. And then Jeanette went missing and we started looking for her. It was all just a coincidence that Jeanette and Cole ended up connected in the end.

Inside the letter is the last will and testament of Desmond Alexander Cole, leaving everything that he owns to his daughter, Karina Davies. Along with the will he left a letter detailing everything, explaining how her mother hadn't wanted her to know about him. About the time they had together. How they both had decided it was for the best that she be raised without knowing him.

He talks about how he always kept an eye on her until he lost all contact when she was around 12. The letter details how sorry he is to have never known her and that he's planning on reconnecting with her, but if something happens, he wants her to know how much he loves her mother and her. It was his love of her mother that kept Cole from ever marrying.

There's also information for his private lawyer, and the private investigator he hired to find her. I'm not sure why neither hadn't come forward during Wright trying to claim her inheritance, but Cadence's theory is that they were waiting for her to make a move first.

It's like something out of a fairy tale and I'm still having a hard time wrapping my head around it. I can just imagine the disbelief Mrs. Davies must be feeling.

"The lawyer can probably help to verify everything." I say.

"He wanted to be sure before he showed it to you." Evan adds.

Darryl was worried about upsetting her if it turned out to be some kind of cruel joke. It *was* rather hard to believe, after all.

"I just can't... this... is this real? I-I never knew. Momma never even hinted that Daddy might not be my dad." She says, staring at the only photo ever taken of her and her biological father. A grainy much folded wallet-sized photo of a young Desmond Cole holding a tiny baby. "Just because the biology is different, doesn't change that he was still my father." She says.

"Just means you had love from two different fathers, they just showed it differently," Cadence says with a whimsical smile. I can practically see the wheels in his brain turning, this'll probably end up in one of his stories.

Mrs. Davies readily agrees and goes to get juices for all of us. We spend the rest of the visit telling stories about Darryl. Well, they tell them. I listen, for the most part.

When we finally leave Darryl's house I turn to both Evan and Cadence as we work to load Evan's wheelchair in the trunk of the car. I've been mulling over a decision for a while now and it seems like a good time to talk about my final choice. Evan smiles encouragingly at me because he already knows what I'm going to say.

"So, remember when I told you that apparently, I like to act." I start as Cadence manages to get the wheelchair inside the vehicle and shuts the door. I move around to the passenger seat.

"Yeah, you said you'd auditioned for something?" Cadence asks, raising both his brows in my direction.

"I'm going to be playing Helena in *A Midsummer Night's Dream* in December. Rehearsals start soon, so I'm going to need a ride."

Cadence doesn't seem so surprised but just smiles and heads toward the library.

"I think I'll ask Risa out." He says suddenly.

"Wait... the library girl?" Evan asks.

"Did you know her?" I ask turning towards Evan.

"Not really... but lover boy... he has been trying to muster up the courage to talk to her for a year now. Made us spend most of our study sessions there."

"Yes, I finally talked to her. Leary over here broke the ice for me." Cadence says.

"Well, I'm all for standing in the background and cheering you on, just try not to be so creepy when you ask her. You want her to say yes."

"I'm not creepy."

"You are definitely creepy."

I start recapping some of Cadence's best moments with Risa and have Evan laughing so hard that there are tears rolling down his cheeks.

We have the windows rolled down and wind is blowing our hair into tangles. I smooth the wrinkles out of my yellow shorts. The laughter, the open road, the warmth of the sun streaming in through the windshield. This all feels familiar.

I am Lyric Lysanne Lyons.

I am 16.

I have four brothers, two loving parents, a best friend that just woke up from a coma, and a doting dog.

I don't remember much of my past, maybe I never will, but I don't think that's such a bad thing anymore. Old Lyric and new Lyric are still me, and I'm still getting to know whoever that is.

Acknowledgements

This book was a labor of love, and hate, and sleepless nights. As any author will say, there's a lot of work that goes into making a book, and it doesn't happen alone.

A special thanks to my parents for always letting me ramble and reading my drafts to give me feedback. For always encouraging me to do what I want. For telling me to stop talking about my book and start writing.

I don't think this book would've happened without Madeline. Thanks for telling me to work on it after sharing story ideas one night. Thanks for reading the chapters as I wrote them. You really were the driving force behind this book. And your editing and feedback really helped improve everything.

Thanks to Cally, if you hadn't pushed me to finish *Coalescence* with you, then I probably would never have gotten to this book.

Thank you, Serena, for giving me space to work, for listening to my ideas all these years.

Thanks Caleb for knowing when to stop talking to me whenever I told you I was writing or editing.

And a special thanks to all my wonderful beta readers: Aunt Pam, Debra N., Cole, Madeline (yes, you get more than one thanks).

Thank you to the rest of my friends and family and to anyone that let me ramble, even a little bit, about my book.

I love you all and am grateful for your support.

And thank you to all of you who have purchased and read this book! I really hope you've enjoyed it.

Author's Note

I came up with the idea for this book years before I actually started working on it. It evolved quite a bit over time, into the story you have here. Being my first novel, I hope I did it justice. This had been many years in the making, and you probably wouldn't recognize the original concept as *How Yellow Fades.*

There was a lot of research that went into this story. I tried to be a little more realistic in some terms at the same time I took a little creative liberty in others. I won't bore you with all of the details, but here are some of the most prevalent.

For instance, with Lyric's amnesia. I couldn't find any instances of a person actually *seeing* their memories, but I honestly believe the mind is more than capable of that. Lyric is basically having really vivid flashbacks, continuously. The auditory hallucinations and the light flickering can also be considered signs of her subconscious trying to trigger her memory.

And like most real amnesiac cases, Lyric won't just regain all her memories. The part I changed a bit is that most people with amnesia are less likely to remember events that took place closer to the time of their accident and more likely to remember things from the far past.

As for Evan, I know comas are a common trope in movies and books. I know of several favorites of mine that use someone in a coma. Often if they wake up they're used to reveal a major plot point. And while, arguably, Evan did explain a bit to Lyric, I tried to keep him from being the major reveal, which is also part of why he didn't wake up until much later (you so knew he was going to wake up).

I probably did *most* of my research on comas. I read a lot about the different types of comas and even some personal stories involving them. I think what perhaps shocked/interested me most is that most people in comas don't just wake up perfectly fine and able to walk and talk. Like logically I should've known that, but it's such a common theme in stories that I just hadn't really thought of it.

I know I've read and seen plenty of stories where the person in the coma wakes up seemingly fine as if they'd just had an extended nap. But that is usually never the case.

While I did have Evan come out of the coma a little easy and didn't feature all of the slow awakening/partial consciousness that most go through. And I had him eating a little more normally, I did want to show that he's not okay. He's going to have some struggles and handicaps that he will need to work through.

I know some might not like the séance scene, but I thought it was a nice addition suggested by one of my Betas to show that Evan's not really a ghost and I did look up a few details about them. I tried to make it realistic in terms of the ritual, but as Carren warns, whether you believe in the occult or not, you should never be like Lyric and do them alone.

Hyperkalemia is a real thing, just in case you were wondering, and it can be caused by a number of things such as kidney dysfunction, potassium sifting out of cells and entering blood circulation, and medications. And it really can lead to cardiac arrest.

I hope you enjoyed my little educational rambling and my book. Thank you so much for buying and reading my work. I hope you'll continue to follow Lyric's journey, because it's not over yet.

Much love,
Lana Lowe

About the Author

Lana is a twenty-something that lives in Tennessee, or more accurately her physical body is in Tennessee and her mind is in countless other worlds. She's constantly reading, traveling dimensions, writing, and thinking up new stories. *How Yellow Fades* is her first published novel.

Her family consists of two little dogs, Hamilton and Nivi, an old grumpy cat named Tally, her parents and their three dogs, Roxie, Anastacia, Banjo, and another, much nicer, cat named Noelle. There are more animals than people and that's just how she likes it.

If you enjoyed this book and want to send feedback, or if you didn't enjoy this book and would like to tell her why, or if you just want to share pictures of your pets, then feel free to send her an email at NightlyEclipsePublications@gmail.com. She'd love to hear from you!

Made in the USA
Lexington, KY
21 December 2018